SECRETS MY MOTHER NEVER TOLD ME

Angela D. Evans

authorHOUSE®

AuthorHouse™
1663 Liberty Drive
Bloomington, IN 47403
www.authorhouse.com
Phone: 1-800-839-8640

Published by AuthorHouse   2/20/2012

ISBN: 978-1-4685-5489-2 (sc)
ISBN: 978-1-4685-5488-5 (e)

Library of Congress Control Number: 2012902981

CHAPTER 1

Innocence

Monic walked into the doctor's office. She gave her name to the receptionist. The receptionist greeted her and told Monic to have a seat. As Monic waited to be called she picked through magazines near by. She finally decided on a woman's magazine with children on the front cover. It portrayed a loving family with two children who had been adopted. Monic looked at the family. They seemed so happy. She wondered if they truly were.

Monic's name was called. She looked up. Monic acknowledged that she heard her name. She returned the magazine where she had found it and stood up. Monic walked over to the woman who had called her. She was lead to a room towards the back of the building. When she entered the room the Psychiatrist greeted her with her hand out. Monic took it and was asked to have a seat. Monic joked asking should she lay down. The psychiatrist told her only if she felt comfortable doing it.

The doctor asked: "So Monic why did you come here today?"

"I came because I need answers."

"Answers to what?"

"My life."

"What kind of answers?"

"Answers to why I'm here, why I had to go through what I did and if I'm my father's child."

"Why do you think you're here? Why do you think you went through what you did? What did you go through? Who do you think you are?"

"I don't know. Where should I start?"

"I think you should start at the place where you're confused the most."

"That's my whole life."

"Then start from your very first memory."

"When I was five years old my mother died of Cancer. It was like one day she just faded away. Like she wasn't real." Monic's voice cracked. She was quiet for a second. When she gained composure Monic cleared her throat and started again.

"My mother and I were living with her boyfriend. The man that I once called my husband."

The doctor looked at Monic with a confused look.

"My biological father had left when she was first diagnosed with terminal cancer. He said that he didn't want to live day to day with death. After he left my mother got a second job. My mother worked hard. I was often left home alone."

"What about relatives?

"As far as I know my mother was an only child. I never met my grandparents. I don't know if they were dead or if my mother was just not speaking to them. My mother never told me much about them. Sometimes she would cry at night and I would hold her. I tried to comfort her, but I was too little. Sometimes my mother would wake up and tell me that she dreamt of her parents. She would smile. My mother would say that her mother and father would be in the house that she grew up in. She and her parents would be sitting on a porch looking out into the street. It was Summer and a block party was going on. She said that her father would stand up and hold his hands out to her mother. She would take his hand and they would begin to dance. She said that sometimes she would interrupt them and get in the middle. She would laugh at it. My mother would say that the sad thing about it was that she didn't know if it was an actual memory or if it was just a dream. Then my mother would get sad. I would ask her where was her mother and father, but she would never say. When she realized I got sad my mother would hug me and say no worries. I would smile up at her. I loved my mother so much. My mother would get up and then get ready for work. She would go over the same rules each time before she left, not to answer the door, not to turn the oven on and to be good.

When my mother left I would turn on the television and watch it all day. Sometimes in the Summer I would sneak and peak out of the window and watch the neighborhood kids playing. Sometimes I wanted to go out to play with the other kids but I was afraid. I always obeyed my mother. She taught me how to prepare peanut butter and jelly sandwiches. On good days there were fruit snacks I could eat on before she came home to make dinner. When my mother came home she would cook dinner. We didn't have much and sometimes my mother ate very little so I could get enough to eat.

We did alright for a while. Then my mother began getting sicker and she didn't have any insurance so she wasn't able to see a specialist. She tried going to the clinic as much as possible, when she wasn't working and she had the $10.00 for the visit. She wasn't able to get much treatment because she didn't have any money. My mother was often sick many times not being able to go in to work, or she would get there and she would have to leave. She soon lost her job. This made it more difficult for her to buy us food. We didn't have much food and eventually she wouldn't eat, giving me all of the food and telling me that she didn't want any food because she was sick. I think she didn't eat a lot of the times because we didn't have enough food and my mother didn't want me to be hungry. You know I would rather have starved if it would have kept her here.

Soon there were people calling my mother all the time upsetting her. This is until our phone got turned off. At that time I didn't know what was going on, but I later realized that they were bill collectors. The phone getting cut off wasn't so bad because that kept my mother from getting those annoying calls. I thought the silence was better. Soon the landlord began banging on the door asking for the rent. My mother would tell me to keep quiet and not to answer the door. I would get very close to her and hug her because after we would hear him walk away my mother would begin to cry.

After months of this, early one morning there was a knock on the door. My mother told me to open it. When I opened it a man entered the apartment. This man handed my mother a piece of paper and told her that she had to leave. He told her that she had four hours to leave the apartment. He said that because of me he would give her a little more time. My mother had one suitcase. She gathered what she could of our clothes and we left our apartment. My mother went to the welfare office and they said she needed an address to get assistance. They gave my mother a piece of paper with an address. It was to a shelter. My mother and I left the office and headed to the shelter.

When we got to the shelter my mother handed them the paper from the welfare office. They took the paper and then directed my mother towards the back of the building. There were two cots, but we shared hers. My mother was so young and even though she was ill she was very beautiful. Some of the men staying in the shelter would try to bother her at night and she was afraid to sleep. She would hold on to me to make sure nothing happened to me. During the warm dry nights my mother found shelter in dark alleyways hidden from the public and we would sleep there. I think she slept better those nights. Sometimes I would wake up and see rats eating food out of the bends. I tried to move being careful not to wake my mother, because I didn't want them to come by us. I guess my mother was so protective of me that she would hold me tight.

One night while my mother was going through a restaurant garbage a man came out of the restaurant. He smiled and spoke to us. He had a kind face. He gave my mother some money. My mother hesitantly took it. It was $20.00. I still remember how happy that made my mother. She thanked him. After the man left me and my mother ate the food that she had gotten out of the bend.

There were a few more times that the man appeared and gave my mother money. Each time she thanked him. There were some days that she found money in the bin. When my mother had gotten enough money we sometimes stayed in motels. She tried to clean them up as much as possible and we carried bug spray to try not to get ate up.

This went on for some time with my mother getting weaker. One night while sleeping in the back of the restaurant the man that had been giving my mother money showed up. He asked my mother if she wanted to stay with him. My mother looked at him suspiciously. The man said that he had a home and several bedrooms. He assured her that she would not have to do anything except keep the house clean. She told him that she was sick and that there would be some days that she wouldn't be able to. The man looked at me and said I'm sure your little one can help you. He smiled and said that she need not worry about that. The man continued smiling and held out his hand. Hesitantly my mother took his hand. He helped her up. My mother was very weak and could barely walk, so the man lifted her into his arms. I thought wow, this is prince charming. You see my mother often told me fairy tales. I thought my mother was now Cinderella or Snow White being rescued by a handsome prince and taken to our castle.

In a short time the man became a friend. My mother's friend took us in. He was very patient with my mother. I tried to do what I could. Some nights when I was put to bed I would hear my mother and the prince talking. When she wasn't feeling too bad they would stay up and watch movies. I would hear them laughing. I began viewing the prince as my father.

After several months of living there my mother moved into his bedroom. Sometimes I would hear my mother tell him that she loved him.

When she got worst he moved her into a guest room. He took good care of her, but I paid the price."

"How is that?"

"It wasn't long before he began visiting me. After giving my mother her medicine and waiting for her to fall asleep he would come into my room. He said that I had to make up for my mother. He said that my mother would want me to fill in and make him happy for giving us a place to stay.

"Did you tell your mother?"

"No. I knew I had to help my mother. We had a nice warm place to stay and my mother couldn't go back to living the way we did before the prince. After my mother died he went to court and was given custody of me."

"No one petitioned?"

"There wasn't anyone. He didn't know my father's name. He never signed my birth certificate. My mother had died and he had the death certificate. He told them that he was all I knew and had. They didn't question it?

For five years we lived as husband and wife. I got my period at nine. Although it was sometimes painful I looked forward to it. My husband wouldn't touch me during that time. Soon after I began getting my period it stopped. I thought that I was sick. My husband noticed that I hadn't gotten it. He went out and got a test and instructed me how to use it. We waited me sitting on the hedge of the tub. My father read it and said that he couldn't believe that I had gotten myself pregnant. I just sat there feeling bad. I was ten years old. I didn't know how I had done it. I told him that I was sorry. My husband/father took me out of school. He told them that we were moving. The first five months I thought maybe I was sick because no baby had come and I was staying home. I read whatever I could that was in the house. The next few months my stomach began growing. I know my father said that I was pregnant, but being my age I really didn't know what that meant and I thought that it might mean that I was dying. Sometimes I had cramps and thought that maybe I had what my mother had. The first time my stomach moved I cried. I didn't know what was going on. I told my husband and he just said that the baby was in there moving around. After that I would just stare at it. I still didn't understand.

The night I went into labor I called out to my mother. I was in so much pain. I thought this is it. I was going to die that night. I was at home alone and my water broke. Me being ten, I didn't know what to do, so I sat in the corner of the den for my husband to come home. He was late that night. By the time he came home the baby's head was hanging from between my legs. My body knew what to do. He heard me scream and came running into the room. He yelled, "What did you do?" I told him that I wet myself and the baby began to come. He told me to shut up. I tried not to scream. I was in so much pain. He told me to lay down. I obeyed. He began pulling the baby out. When the baby came out, I remembered it being silent. I thought how good the baby was, it knew to be quiet.

Later I found out that the baby died. I was too young

to have the baby. My body wasn't ready and I held the baby in too long after my water broke. In a way I was sad, but then it was a relief. The baby was a girl and I was too young to be in that situation. Deep within I felt my baby girl had been spared.

After two weeks my body had gone back to the way it had been before I was pregnant. It went back to me looking like a ten year old body again and my husband placed me in a different school. I was so far behind the other students. My father helped me with my homework. He said that he wasn't raising a dummy. When I wasn't cooking and cleaning I was studying. On the nights that I wasn't fulfilling my wifely duties I stayed up late to study. I loved reading and history was my favorite subject. I loved school. It was a way to escape my life.

Some days going to school was hard in the beginning. I had just had my baby girl and my breast was engorged with milk, which made my breast pretty big at times. I wore bigger clothes for a while until they went down and the milk stopped coming. The few kids that noticed those days thought that I was putting tissue in my bra to make my breast bigger. They sometimes teased me. I did actually have tissue in my bra, not to make them larger, but to keep them from wetting my shirts up. I can see why they were confused, so was I.

On the normal days my breast was small, like a typical ten year old. I didn't know what was going on with me, because my husband would just tell me it was woman stuff. When I would get my period my father would get me pads. Once he got me tampons. He got them too big and I couldn't sit down because it hurt too bad; so he started getting me pads.

Surprisingly I had one best friend. My father would sometimes let me visit with her at her house for a few hours after school. That's if he expected to be home late. Then I would have to get home. I would never invite her over to my home. I would tell her that my father didn't like people to come to visit. She never pressed it and I was happy. The times that I spent with my friend was when I felt my age. It was wonderful. I sometimes got to go to the movie theater with her. We laughed at comedies, screamed at scary movies and cried at sad ones. You know I even had a fantasy of Prince Charming.

My husband was good to me. He owned our home. He even let me decorate it. I used the Good House Keeping magazines to get ideas. When my husband came home in the evening I had his slippers ready at the door. He was a creature of habit. He was home at the same time every evening. I would be waiting at the front door with his slippers. If he wore a coat I would take it and kiss him hello. After hanging it up, I would come into the dinning room where he would be sitting, waiting for me to serve him. I would get our plates and place food on them. I would give him his food and then place wine down. I would pour him a glass of wine and me grape juice. He didn't like women to drink. We would pray and then begin to eat.

As we ate my father would ask me how school was. I would tell him about my day. He would look so proud when I told him that I made an "A" on my test or homework.

After dinner I cleaned up the kitchen. When I was finished with the kitchen I would go into our bathroom and run a bath for my husband and me. He would sit behind me and tell me about his day. If I was on my period I would bathe alone. I enjoyed those seven days. He wouldn't touch me. Those were the only days. I often wondered how he felt like having sex every night. Sometimes I used to think that maybe that's why my mother died. My mother and father use to have sex every night until she was too weak and that's when he started visiting me. After I had my baby my husband was more careful. He bought over the counter stuff for me to prepare before we had sex. My father made sure I cleaned myself well.

CHAPTER 2

Childhood

In fifth grade I graduated at the top of my class. The school had a class trip to Six Flags and my friend's mother threw a sleep over for that weekend. Surprisingly my father let me go. I was so excited that I didn't sleep the night before the trip. When the bus departed I waved at my husband and father. I fantasized of going far away and not coming back. I watched the other cars that we passed. I was kind of disappointed when we stopped at Six Flags. All the kids jumped off the bus excitedly. I eventually joined in the excitement. We rode on all of the rides that our height would permit. We played some of the games. I didn't win anything. Five hours later we were heading back to the bus. I got sad and then my friend said that her mother would be at the school to pick us up. I remembered that I wasn't going home for the weekend and that I get to be a kid a little longer. Not having any responsibility was great.

When we got to my friend's house me and ten other

girls danced, ate and then they began to talk about boys. I kept quiet, I knew that they wouldn't understand, heck I didn't understand my life. I giggled, I was ten. The entire weekend we had pillow fights, talks about boys, danced, went swimming and just played little girl games. As the weekend drew to a close I became sad again. I knew that my reality was coming back soon. My friend Lori's mother drove me back home. I thanked Mrs. Banks and slowly got out of the car. When I got up to my porch I looked back and waved. I then went into my reality.

It was 5 O'clock. I went up to my bedroom. I looked around, nothing in it spoke of my age. I placed my bags down. On my dresser mirror was a note. It said welcome home sweetheart. I'll be home at seven. I knew what that meant. I began cooking. When it was done I got my husband's slippers. He had kept the house clean and school was out so I didn't have anything to do, so I waited sitting in front of the door with my legs folded. When I heard the key I jumped up. I stood there until he came in. After he closed the door he hugged me as if he missed me. I hugged him back, thinking of how I was missing out on fun. After he released me he took off his shoes and I placed the slippers on his feet. He put his arm around me and we walked into the dinning room. He sat down and I did my usual routine. We ate dinner. After dinner I cleaned the kitchen and then went up to our bedroom. He told me to run the shower. That was the first time that we took a shower. I prefer showers. He washed me. It was different. It was as if he was trying to wash off the past weekend. After my gentle scrub he dried me off and carried me to bed. He whispered he missed me in my ear.

I was happy when he was finished so I could go to sleep and dream about the weekend that I was ten........

The summer proved to be fun. My father let me go to away camp. It was for three weeks. The day that I was to go I had my bags packed and by the front door. That morning my father drove me to the bus. I kissed my father on the cheek and ran to the bus. I was so afraid that my husband would change his mind. He waited until the bus was out of site. As the bus drove away I watched, still afraid that he would stop the bus and take me off. When we were out of site a boy on the bus, named Winfred came up to me. He said hi and then asked was this my first time. I looked at him bewildered. He repeated himself. "Is this your first away camp?" I said yes. He said, "My name is Winfred and I'm a pro. I've been going away every summer since I was eight."

I thought Wow!

He said, "I'll show you around and take care of you."

We didn't have co-ed rooms, but Winfred and I spent whatever time we could during the day. Everyday we went swimming and played camp games. A couple of times we snuck out at night and sat at the base of the lake. I had never had so much fun. Each day I woke up with excited expectancy. Winfred and I challenged other kids to races and all types of other games that we could think of. We ate all of our meals together.....

The last few days of camp Winfred asked me to be his girlfriend. I looked at him again bewildered. He said, "I like you. We don't have to tell anyone." I didn't know what to say. I felt like I was cheating on my husband. A word I didn't know until later in life. I just stood there dumbfounded. He said that if my father was strict that I could call him when my father wasn't around. I didn't know how to be a girlfriend. I had a husband. I knew I couldn't tell him about that. I asked him how do I be a girlfriend. He told me that we talk on the phone and maybe one day go out to a movie. Then he asked if he could kiss me. I moved back. He thought that I was scared. I was afraid, but not because it was my first kiss. I was married and this was the first kiss from an eleven year old boy. My husband was thirty. Winfred moved closer to me. He clumsily kissed me on the lips. It was quick and with his mouth closed. Although it was something less than what I was used to and not what I expected I rather enjoyed what I viewed as my first kiss.

The day we left I became sad. We sat next to each other and vowed to stay in touch. He lived in Newark and me in West Orange. He gave me his phone number. I shakily gave him mine. I instructed him the times that he could call.

A couple of blocks away I changed my seat.

When we pulled into the parking lot I saw my father's car. I slowly got off the bus. He remained by the car. I carried my bag to the car. He hugged me and kissed me like a loving father. He picked up my bag and placed it in the back seat. We got into the car. He asked me what I had done at the camp. Well you know I couldn't tell him about Winfred, so I told him everything changing Winfred to Wendy. He seemed to be pleased with what I had told him. When we arrived home he got my bag and we went into the house. For the first time he ordered pizza. We sat in the T.V. room, watched movies and ate the pizza. When we got ready to go up to our room he told me that he had fixed up my room. I looked at him puzzled. He told me that there were going to be some changes. I will not be sleeping in our room anymore. I was confused, but overjoyed. When I went into my room all of my clothes were in there. That night I laid in what was my own bed, alone. I stretched out elated that my father was home. I woke up a few times during the night expecting my husband to come to invade my room, but he didn't.

The next few weeks I got ready for school. I felt like a kid. It was strange; because there were very few times I had felt that way.

When I returned to school I saw my best friend. She told me about her summer. This year I was proud and could hardly wait for her to finish telling her stories. When it was my turn, I bragged about my camp adventure and proudly said that I had a boyfriend during the Summer. She and her friends stared at me, looking to see if I was pulling their leg. I was big stuff. I felt different now. My husband had gone away for almost two months. Sometimes I wondered, but was overjoyed that I didn't have to be a wife. I still cooked, but I brought my father his slippers and not my husband. We had nice conversations about what I was doing in school. After dinner I went up to my room and took showers alone.

CHAPTER 3

Adolescence

My birthday was coming up and my father asked me what I wanted for my birthday. I really didn't know what to say, because I was afraid that my husband would come back. I cautiously asked him if I could have a party at a hotel. I didn't want anyone to come to my home. I was still protective of other children. To my surprise and delight my father agreed to it. He even let Lori's mother chaperon. I told him that she would even bring me home. He told me that was fine and that he and I would cut a cake before I leave for my eleventh birthday party. I was so happy. I was excited, because I managed to get in touch with Winfred. He was there with a flower in his hand. I hugged him. We danced all night. They sang happy birthday to me and I opened my gifts. For the first time I was given age appropriate gifts.

When the party was over, for the first time I didn't dread going home. Mrs. Banks dropped me home. I

happily picked up all of my gifts and skipped to my front
door.

When I went to open the door he was waiting. When
I closed the door he hugged me and asked if I had a good
time. I nervously said yes, not sure if my husband had
come back. I smiled when he said, "Let me take your
gifts to your room." When I got in my room and the
door closed I spin around. I then got in my bed and fell
fast asleep.

The next morning I woke up. I got dressed and
quickly ran down to the kitchen to prepare breakfast. To
my surprise there was a young woman, my guest eighteen,
dressed in lingerie cooking. I stood in the doorway
speechless. She turned and said, "Hi Monic." I continued
to stand in the doorway. My father came up behind me.
He was wearing a silk house coat. He said, "Hi Monic,
this is my wife Stephanie." I was going to tell you last
night, but I figured I'd do it over breakfast." I know it
sounds weird, but I was kind of jealous, but then again I
was ecstatic that I was no longer a wife. Somehow I had
been divorced. I thought wow my eleventh birthday was
great and now I can be a kid. Stephanie will be cleaning,
cooking and would have to have sex with my husband.

Enthusiastically I said, "Hi."

Stephanie said, "You can call me Stephanie."

I was fine with this. That night I over heard them.
Stephanie was calling my father's name. She seemed to like
having sex with him. I started thinking that something
was wrong with me for not enjoying it. Then I thought
maybe he loves his third wife more than me because he
made her feel good. I kind of resented her for that, but I
was never rude to her.

Monday came and for the first time I didn't have to prepare breakfast. It was ready when I came down stairs. Stephanie even asked me if I wanted her to prepare lunch. I told her no. When I came home Stephanie was sitting in the T.V. room. She asked me how my day was. I thought that was nice. She then told me that my father had left instructions on how he liked things in his home. I told her how everything had to be and about his slippers......

Months went by and life was wonderful. I got to visit my friends and my only chore was to clean my room. I got my own phone. I talked with Winfred. I kept this a secret. Only me and my best friend Lori knew of this.

Stephanie was fun. When my father was not there she and I talked. We played games. She would tell me about her old boyfriends. She told me about sex. I was shocked. I had been having sex for five years and didn't know the first thing about it. I giggled when she told me about orgasms. She told me how to know when I had one. In all my years I had never had one. I thought maybe I was still a virgin. Then I thought of my baby. She confided that she and my father hadn't actually gotten married in the legal since. She told me that she met my father during the summer. They met the first night that I had gone to away camp. He had gone out to a club. Their eyes met and he had brought her home. He told Stephanie that he had a little girl and that he had been alone for a long time; that his daughter was in away camp. Stephanie said that she doesn't usually go home with men the first night, but my father looked lonely. She said that she didn't intend to sleep with him, but he was very attractive and when he kissed her it sent chills up her spin. I thought to myself, what was wrong with me. I never felt that. Stephanie must have sensed my confusion because she said, "When you meet that special guy you'll feel all the things that I've told you I feel." Then she nudged me and said there might be a few guys who may make me feel that way. I guess I looked like I doubted it so she said, "You'll see."

When it would get close to my father coming home we would get in position. Stephanie would go to prepare dinner and I would go up to my room and do my homework. When my father came in the door I could hear Stephanie greet him. She not only had his slippers, but she added a hug and a kiss that I couldn't imagine doing. Watching it made me think, wow she really loves him. I questioned if I really loved my husband. I was happy that now my husband had a woman who would really love him and make him happy. I guess my father was here now. Things were really great now. I got to be my age. Stephanie was not like a mother, she was more like a big sister. I also thought of her as my hero because she made it possible for me to be a child.

A year went by and my birthday was here again. Stephanie managed to throw me a surprise birthday party. I was twelve now and this was the first time I had ever had any one at my house. She made it so nice. Stephanie had balloons with happy birthday on them throughout the house and some of them even had my name on them. She had a sheet cake with the same sentiment on it. It was decorated with things that a twelve year old would like. Twelve candles were on it. I was happy. I had a great time, but part of me had an uneasy feeling. The only face that I didn't see was Winfred's. He hadn't been invited because he was a secret. I didn't see any sign of my father at the party. We played games and danced all during the party.

When it was time to cut the cake my father came down and everyone sang happy birthday. I was happy when my father went back upstairs.

At the end of the night I thanked everyone for coming. I said goodbye and went up to my room and called Winfred. I told him about the party and said that I was sorry that he had not been there. We talked a while and then I went to bed.

The next morning I hugged Stephanie and thanked her. She hugged me back, but she seemed different. This scared me. I didn't know if something happened at the party or if it was things between her and my father. I worried that I would have to become the wife again. I tried to help out around the house more to relieve Stephanie of some of her chores, because I was afraid that she would leave us.....

As time past my father would go out often, leaving Stephanie alone with me. Sometimes I would hear him come home late and Stephanie would be crying. She would tell him that she loved him and asked him why he didn't love her any more. He would tell her that she was getting old. I couldn't believe what he was saying. She was only nineteen. I tried to stay out of my father's site as much as possible.

Christmas was sad. My father was out late, which had become his normal behavior. Stephanie asked me for a hug. I began to cry. She went up to their room. I knew what this meant. She was the closes I had since my mother, who I could hardly remember now. I sat on the bottom of the stairs. She was only up there a few minutes when I saw her come back down with two bags. I guess she had packed earlier. I heard a horn blow and then Stephanie headed to the door. I ran after her and begged her to stay. She looked at me and said that she couldn't, that she was unhappy and my father didn't want her any more. As she walked out the door she looked back and said that if I ever needed her to call. Before she closed the door I ran up behind her, hugged her around the waist and cried. She turned around and hugged me. She said that she wished that she could take me, but she didn't know where she was going. Stephanie also promised that she wasn't leaving me, she was leaving my father. She said goodbye and left. I ran up to my room and cried all night.

The next day my father came home. He came into my room and asked where Stephanie was. I told him that she had left. He said fine and walked out the door. I heard him moving things around in his room. I became afraid. I didn't want to be the wife again. I spent most of the two weeks of Christmas vacation alone at home. I was happy my husband was out and often listened late at night hoping he wouldn't come back.

After the two weeks were over my father came home. He was not alone. He had a girl who was fifteen years old with him. He said Monic this is my girlfriend, Cynthia. He looked at the girl and said, "Maybe one day you will be my wife." By the smile of Cynthia I figured that she might be trouble. Again I was instructed to teach her the way the house should be run. Although I didn't feel comfortable with Cynthia, I still was very nice to her. I was actually happy that she was there, so I wouldn't have to be the wife. Sometimes I felt bad for her. She wasn't much older than me. Sometimes she walked as if she was in pain and some nights I would hear her yelling saying it hurt. I couldn't and didn't imagine what they were in there doing.

One night several months later I was helping Cynthia clean their bedroom. She didn't look like she was feeling well. I told her to go to my room and lay down, that I would take care of the house. As I was cleaning their room I began to take the sheets off the bed. The sheets had blood on them. I thought maybe she had gotten her menstruation. I continued pulling the sheets off. When I went into the linen closet in their room I discovered some sex tapes. Curious I put the tape in. I couldn't believe what I was seeing. The men were doing things to women I would have never thought possible. I put the tape back and finished cleaning their room. After finishing the house I had a few hours before my father would be home. I went into my room. Cynthia was laying on my bed bald up and shaking. I asked her was she ok. She just looked at me. I asked her if she was menstruating. She said no. She reached out her hand. I moved in closer and took her hand. I asked what's wrong. She was bleeding from her behind. Stupidly even though I had just seen the tapes I asked why. She looked at me and I knew. I helped her into the bathroom. I called Planned Parent Hood. I had learned this from Stephanie. I told them that I had a friend who had anal sex and that she was bleeding. They told me to try to get my friend to go to the doctor. I was scared about going, because I didn't want my father to come home and we not be there.

I called a cab to save time and convinced Cynthia that we would be back in time. We got to the clinic. After waiting just a little while Cynthia was called in. She asked if I could go in. They allowed it. I stood by her side while

the doctor examined her. We found out that there was a
tare in Cynthia's rectum. The doctor assured her that it
would heal. They gave her birth control, pamphlets and
medicine for her rectum. She was instructed not to have
sexual intercourse until it healed.

Still afraid of what my father would say we kept the
secret between the two of us. We hid everything in my
room. We rushed around the house, or I rushed and
Cynthia helped as much as she could, being in pain and
all.

When my father came home she was at the door
smiling as much as she could through the pain. She held
his slippers in hand. As she bent down she moaned. My
father asked her if he had hurt her. She lied and smiled a
little. He kissed her and said he didn't mean to.

We quietly ate dinner that night. I volunteered to
clean the kitchen. My father seeing Cynthia in pain told
her she could go up stairs early and to be ready by nine. I
couldn't believe he wasn't going to let her get better.

At nine my curiosity got the better of me. I turned off
the radio in my room. I cracked my door and listened. At
first I heard my father turn on their television and then
I heard sounds. I realized that it was the women in the
movies. Then I heard my father tell Cynthia to do what
the woman was doing. I heard moaning and my father
saying that's it. I remembered a scene in the movie. I
grabbed my mouth. Then I heard him tell her to get up.
Surprisingly I heard her call out his name and say that she
loved him. I closed my door and turned my radio back
on. I laid there thinking how could she love him and it
was unthinkable, but she actually sounded as if she was
enjoying it. I was so confused.

The next day I returned to school. I had so many questions and no one to ask. I got a pass to the library and I checked out books about sex and the body. I hid them when I got home. Cynthia seemed to be feeling better. She was singing when I came into the kitchen. I didn't know how to ask and she wasn't much older than I, but I couldn't resist. I told her that I had gone to get something to eat last night and I over heard her telling my father that she loved him. She explained to me that she did love him and that he made her feel so good. I must have looked confused. She explained that she didn't concentrate on her behind and that she had taken some of the pain killers the clinic had given her. I accepted her answer, but I was still confused.

After dinner I read the books that I had rented from the library and looked at the few pictures in the books. This helped, but I doubted if I could ever feel the way Stephanie, Cynthia and how the book said I would feel.

As time past Cynthia seemed to change. She would give me a look of resentment. I didn't know why. I was very nice to her. I was happy that she was there, because I could live my life. Sometimes she would say negative things to me. I ignored them. No matter what, I didn't want her to leave.....

One day I came home from school. Cynthia was waiting at the door. I was surprised, because normally she would be upstairs in their room or in the kitchen. She said he loves you. I asked her what she was talking about. She said that he calls my name when he's having sex with her. My face went pale. For a minute she looked concerned. She asked me was I ok. I told her that he probably was concerned about me, that I was sure he didn't mean it. She looked at me and the concern went out of her face. She asked me if I was sure. I told her of course. She said that was what he told her, but she didn't believe him until now. I was relieved. I reinforced that he loved her and told her that he would be crushed if she was to leave. I also added that I would miss her. The only thing is that I wouldn't miss her because I liked her so much, it was because I didn't want to go back to my past life. Everyday I would tell Cynthia that I was happy that she was here.

his house. When we got there we went up to his room. He still holding my hand closed the door. He turned on slow music and then walked me over to the bed. He sat down on the bed and pulled me to sit on his lap. We began to kiss. He leaned back placing me on top of him. He asked me was I frightened. I wasn't sure. This wasn't my first time having sex. My quietness made him think that I was afraid. He told me not to be. We kissed. He put his hand on my behind and told me to move with him. He squeezed my behind. I felt something. After a while I felt him under me vibrate and then I felt myself feel something. I thought to myself could this be what Stephanie was talking about. He kissed me harder and then he moved me off of him. He went into the bathroom. I sat there amazed and feeling different. I thought, "So this is it. My first." When Dennis returned he said do you know what you made me do. I told him no, wanting to hear him say it. "You made me feel good." He asked me if I felt good and I said yes. I actually did. I didn't feel weird any more. We continued this for a few months. I looked forward to us getting together.

Back at home Cynthia and my father were happy. All was well.

Two months past. My father came home early. I was surprised. He and Cynthia went up to their room. He asked her why she had asked him to come home. After a few minutes of silence she told him that she was pregnant. Again it was silent. They came downstairs and called me down. He told me to sit down. I sat down. He said, "There is going to be an addition to the family. Cynthia is pregnant." I sat there not able to verbalize my feelings. I managed to say great. I hugged Cynthia.

At dinner everyone was quiet. I had never been so happy to go up to my room.

Fear came over me. Some of the fear that I felt was not only for me, but for Cynthia and her baby. I was afraid that my husband would return. I was afraid for the baby if it was a girl and I was afraid that he would not find Cynthia attractive any more and she would leave. I was confused as to whether to help her around the house so she wouldn't loose the baby or if I wanted her to lose it.....

For the next few weeks I helped out. Cynthia said that she was ok and I could go on with being with my friends. I guess Cynthia felt something because she began to exercise. Her body actually looked better at four months than it had before she was pregnant. She ate, but watched eating too much. I could tell that my father was actually more attracted to her with her new tight body. This made me happy. I knew all was well.....

On my fourteenth birthday I pretended that Lori and I were going to a party and that I wanted to spend the night at her house. My father approved it. Dennis' parents were going away and he would be home alone for two days....

I left early that morning and went over Dennis' house. He met me as usual at the bus stop. When we got to his house we went up to his room as usual. He told me that he wanted us to watch a movie. He told me to lay on the bed. I obeyed. I was ready for our usual rubbing. He turned on the T.V. and placed a tape in the VCR. I couldn't believe he had a tape like this.

At first I was afraid. Afraid that he was going to want

me to do some nasty crazy thing, but it was a mild tape. It was weird, but they weren't too many crazy things.

As we watched Dennis said that he wanted to try something different. I was nervous, but we had been seeing each other for a year now and I was fourteen now. I said ok. We continued to watch the tape. Dennis took off my blouse. He watched the tape and mimic what he saw. Surprisingly I liked it. Then the man on the tape took the woman's bottom garments off, revealing her thong panties and stockings. He left these on. Dennis told me that next time he wanted me to wear something like that. I told him that I didn't know if I could get them. He begged me to try. I said that I would. Dennis took off my pants leaving my bikini panties on. I layed there in my underwear. I could tell by his pants that he was aroused. He started kissing me and touching my breast. After touching my breast he moved down to my panties. He still watched the movie as he touched me. He followed the movie step by step. I had never felt like that. He continued until my body began to jerk uncontrollably. He smiled and asked if I liked it. I embarrassingly said yes. He kissed me and told me not to be embarrassed, that he wanted to make me feel good.

He laid next to me and began kissing me again. He touched my body once again. I felt myself becoming arouse again. He pulled my panties off and climbed on top of me. I became afraid, because I wondered if this would feel like it did with my husband. Dennis felt my uneasiness. He kissed me and whispered in my ear that he promised it would feel good. I braced myself to accept him, but he stopped himself. He placed himself on me and told me to move with him. I obeyed. We kissed and moved together. Just as our bodies longed to release it's tension Dennis and I became one. He moaned in my ear and both of our bodies burst together. He grabbed my face and kissed me with such passion.

I held onto him not wanting to end that moment. He stayed on top of me and we fell asleep......

The tape had ended, rewind itself and started again when we woke up. Dennis gave me a look and I knew that he wanted to have sex again. Correction, he said that we were making love. I asked him what was the difference. He said having sex doesn't require people to care about each other, but what we were doing was making love because we cared about each other....

Those two days were wonderful. I felt so good, not because of what we did, but how I felt during and afterwards. When it was time for me to leave I became sad. I didn't want to lose that feeling that I felt that weekend. Dennis walked me to the bus stop. When the bus arrived he kissed me and I got on the bus. I looked at him until I couldn't see him anymore......

When I arrived home the house was dark. I looked around downstairs. When I didn't find anyone downstairs I went upstairs. I looked in my room, why I don't know. It was as I left it. I then went cautiously to my father's bedroom. It was dark, but I could see a figure in the bed. Although I was nervous, because I knew something was wrong I ventured in. I flick the light on. There balled up was Cynthia. She was rocking. I walked over to her. I asked her what was wrong. She looked up at me and said it's the baby. Cynthia was five months. It was late. My father hadn't come home yet. I knew that we only had one hour. I was concerned more that Cynthia could really be ill and would be put in the hospital, but I couldn't let her lay here in pain. I called an ambulance. When they came they examined her. They said that she needed to rest. They instructed her not to do anything for a couple of days. I thanked them for coming and told Cynthia I would take care of dinner. When my father came home I was at the door with his slippers. Before he could say or do anything I pointed up the stairs and told him that Cynthia was sick. He patted me on the head and thanked me. He went upstairs......

When he came back he told me to fix a plate and he would take it up to Cynthia. He told me to go on and eat and said good night....

All the while I ate alone I thought of my two days with Dennis. I was happy to be alone. I cleaned the kitchen and was on my way upstairs when I heard noise coming out of my father's room. I listened thinking I know she told him that she was in pain. Then I realized that it was one of his tapes. I went into my room and closed the door. Still mesmerized I laid in my bed with everything off thinking about the way Dennis made me feel. I came back to where I was when I heard Cynthia scream. I jumped. I wasn't sure if I should intervene. I got out of bed and slowly walked towards their bedroom door. The door was partly opened. I was frozen still, not able to move when I saw my father behind Cynthia. I realized that she wasn't screaming mainly from pain, but she was enjoying it. She was yelling out of pleasure not pain. I eased back to my room, careful not to let anyone know that I was out of my room. I turned my music up to block out the sounds. Afterwards instead of thinking about Dennis, I laid there wondering what I saw. I saw how much pain Cynthia was in and being pregnant she shouldn't really be doing anything. She was told to rest, that's not resting. I thought maybe she loves him so much that she can't say no. After my time with Dennis I could appreciate her body craving the pleasure of what Dennis called love making.

The next morning I awakened. I dressed and went downstairs. To my surprise Cynthia was up. She was moving slowly, but she was the wife now and she wanted to please her husband. I understood, not because I loved my husband, but because that is what a wife does, take care of her husband. I gained respect for Cynthia and I was happy that she kept her body in shape so my father would still be attracted to her.

She was five months pregnant and wasn't even showing. She worked out a lot. I thought of working out too. I liked my body at fourteen. My breast were full without being too large. I had a small waist and what Dennis said a nice size behind, not big but not small. I had long legs and my body was tone despite not exercising.

When I walked into the kitchen I spoke and she spoke back. I asked her how she was doing and she said fine. She thanked me for yesterday. I asked her if she wanted me to help and she declined.

After she was finished cooking she prepared the plates for us. She went up to get my father. They came down together. We prayed and then ate. After breakfast I went back up to my room. Cynthia was left by herself to clean the kitchen. My father always sat in the den reading the Sunday paper. I was careful talking with Dennis. He said that he had enjoyed our time together and he couldn't stop thinking of me. He said that he couldn't wait until we could get together again. I told him that I felt the same way.

My father came to the door. He actually knocked. I was so surprised that at first I didn't answer. My father knocked again. I hung up the phone. I sat in the chair by my computer and told my father to come in. He came in. He looked concerned. I asked him if everything was alright. He told me that he had to take Cynthia to the hospital. He didn't say anything else. He left my room. I watched as they left for the hospital. I was concerned that Cynthia would have to stay the night. Then I thought about my father, he would convince them to release her. I stayed up as long as I could. I finally fell asleep. I had not slept much in three days......

I awakened early the next morning. I came out of my room and went down to the kitchen. Sure enough Cynthia was there. I asked her how she was feeling. She said fine. I asked how was the baby, she said that she lost the baby. She looked sad. I remembered my baby and how I felt. I walked over to her and hugged her. Although I was relieved, I was also sorry for her because she really wanted it. I wondered if it had been a boy or girl. I thought that it was probably a girl and that's why it didn't survive, so she wouldn't have to go through what I've been through and even though Cynthia doesn't realize it, it won't have to go through what her mother has had to endure. I told her that they could try again. Cynthia said that my father had them place something in her that would prevent her from getting pregnant for five years......

Well I was coming up on another birthday and so was Cynthia. This frightened me because I was at the age Cynthia was when she came and Cynthia was also turning another year older. We had realized the first year that she came home with my father that she should not celebrate her birthday or at least keep it quiet. Although Cynthia was turning seventeen she dressed much younger and kept herself thin so she would keep looking younger. I felt sorry for her because she truly loved my father.

For my fifteenth birthday I asked if I could have a party at a hotel and me and my friends spend the weekend there. Cynthia wanting to be alone with my father convinced him to let me have it. I told my father that Lori's mother would chaperone like last time. I told my father that I was going over to Lori's house and we would leave from there....

I left Friday morning. I checked into the hotel. I dressed in a provocative outfit and sat nervously as I waited for Dennis.

Dennis arrived an hour after I had gotten there. He knocked on the door. I asked who it was. He said Dennis. I hid behind the door and opened it. I closed the door behind me and placed the extra latch on the door. Dennis walked in. He hadn't noticed what I had on. He walked over to the window. We had a view to the ocean. I went up behind him. I put my arms around him. He went to put his arms behind himself and felt skin. He turned quickly. He looked at me. He asked, "What are you wearing? I became embarrassed and turned my head. He pulled my head up and said I'm sorry. I didn't mean it the way it sounded. He said you look sexy. I just wasn't expecting this. He moved me to the bed. We stayed in the room most of the weekend. We ordered food in. He ordered me a small birthday cake and sang happy birthday to me. I made a wish that we could stay here forever.......

When it was time to return home I cried. I told Dennis that I was in love with him and I didn't want to go back home. He said that I had to, that he cared about me and that we shouldn't rush things. I thought to myself, rush things, there's nothing much left that we hadn't done. Of course this was an exaggeration....

I returned home. It was if I wasn't missed. Cynthia said oh you're back. I looked at her and thought, not by choice. I went up stairs to my room.

Things changed between Dennis and me. He was never available anymore. Many times when I called him his voice mail picked up. At first I would leave messages and then I caught on and would just hang up the phone.....

A month went past and I missed my period. I called Dennis frantic, but again he did not answer the phone and did not return my call. I went to Planned Parenthood. They ran test. I was relieved that I was not pregnant. I remembered what my father did with Cynthia and asked them to place the birth control in me. I swore I would never be in this situation again.

When I got home I called Dennis one last time, maybe out of courtesy or maybe out of anger. I left a message saying that I wasn't pregnant, that it was a false alarm. I hoped to hear from him, but he never called....

As time past I realized that I had frightened him away. I vowed to never reveal my feelings unless I was completely sure that the man felt the same way.

"How did that make you feel?"

"As time past and when you're miserable it past slowly. I finally put Dennis behind me. I began to hang over Lori's house more often. We went to the movies often. Sometimes I would think of Dennis because that's where

I had met him. I began going to a roller skating rink in Branch Brook Park. Lori and I went for it's grand opening. We had so much fun. We made it our point to go every Saturday.

It was teen night. I saw my father parked not far from the rink. He did not see me and no one else that I know of saw him. I at least hoped not. I had been going to the rink every Saturday for a month when I met Carlos. Carlos was eighteen years old. I thought that he was so fine. He would look at me and I would look away.

I had learned to skate pretty good. One particular Saturday I was showing off trying to get Carlos to notice me. When all of a sudden this kid skated pass me. He lost his balance and took me down with him. Carlos saw this and came to my rescue. He said as he helped me up, are you alright. I was so embarrassed that I didn't say anything. He helped me over to the sitting area. When I still had not said anything he said I'm Carlos. I was still in a zone. As he went to walk away I quickly looked up and said thank you. He turned around and said anytime. I said my name is Monic. He walked back to me and sat next to me. He said nice to meet you. We skated together the rest of the night. When the rink closed Carlos offered Lori and me a ride. We normally took the bus. This time we allowed Carlos to drop us off. He took Lori home first. I told Lori that I would be safe.

Carlos drove off. He asked if we could go somewhere to talk. I said sure.

It had been three months now since Dennis and I had made love and my body was yearning to be touched. Carlos drove to a deserted area. He placed his arm on the back of my seat. He had the sexiest smile. We talked for a little while and then he asked me if he could kiss me. I welcomed this because I loved to kiss. Dennis was such a good kisser. Carlos kissed different, but it was still good. We kissed for a while. Then he pulled back. He said that he should get me home. I was surprised and somewhat impressed. He dropped me a block from my home. I told him that I had a strict father. He asked if he could get my number. I gave it to him. I didn't ask for his.

After talking on the phone for a little while he began picking me up after school and we would go to what became our spot. This went on for three months. Summer was here and we had gotten out of school. I volunteered to work in a hospital. Carlos would pick me up from the hospital and we would drive down to the beach. These days my father was coming home late so I didn't worry about time. Carlos and I would lay on the beach and kiss. He never tried to touch me. I wanted him to.

It had been six months since Carlos and I met. We went to the beach. As it got dark and the beach became deserted, Carlos kissed me. For the first time he touched my breast. He was gentle. We kissed for a long time. He continued to caress my breast, even after we stopped kissing. He asked me if it felt good. I said yes. He took the back of his hand and smoothed it down my stomach. He looked at me. When I didn't protest his hand moved further down my body. I tried not to move. It felt so good. After a while he stopped and looked at me again. He kissed me again. This time with more intensity. He removed my top and then my pants. He got on top of me. He continued to kiss me. As he moved on top of me I opened my legs and began to move with him. He removed his pants. We continued to move together. As our bodies longed to be one we granted them and became as one. Carlos was very skilled. When we had been satisfied we went into the bath houses to wash off. Carlos then took me to the usual drop off. We spent our entire summer going to the beach, and made love there every evening after everyone had left.

When the summer was over Carlos returned to college and I returned to high school. I missed Carlos. He was so gentle and caring. We wrote each other every day for a month and then the letters tapered off. I was ok with that. We had never made any promises to each other......

School was back in and I looked forward to seeing my classmates. I saw very little of Lori. I called her on occasion, but between volunteering and writing Carlos I had no time left. I was happy that she had her own things going on......

For my sixteenth birthday Cynthia suggested that I have a sweet sixteen party. I declined."

"Why? That's a very special time in a girl's entry into the world."

"I didn't feel sweet and again I didn't want my father to be a part of my day. I contacted Lori and she was available. Lori, a few other girls and I went to a teen's club. We met some guys there and danced and mingled with them throughout the night. We stayed until the club closed. One of the guys gave me his number. He didn't ask for mine. I never called him.

When I got home that night Cynthia was up. My father had not come home. She told me that this had been the second night. I told her not to worry. I knew that it was plenty to worry about. I really didn't worry about my husband coming back, because I was at an age that he saw as getting old.

Although I looked sixteen I looked older than Cynthia. She had lost a lot of weight trying to look fifteen. I noticed that for each birthday my father had become a little more distant from Cynthia. I tried not to recognize it. I felt bad for Cynthia because she had given up so much.

My father stayed away three more days, making almost a week. The night he came home I heard Cynthia crying. I don't know what he had said to her, but for the next week she walked around in a daze.

I came home early Friday. I went into the kitchen to see how Cynthia was doing. She wasn't there. I heard water running. I knew my father wasn't home. I cautiously, slowly went into my father's room. I saw water on the carpet. I picked up my paste. I went into the bathroom. I stood frozen. There in the tub covered in blood and water was Cynthia. As the water hit my feet I came out of my trance. I ran to the phone and called 911. I turned off the water. I knew my father would be pist.

On the dresser I saw a letter addressed to my father. I can still remember word for word. It read:

"To my husband. The years have been wonderful. I tried to be what you wanted me to be. I failed you. When you came in last night and said that I was old and had become ugly and that you couldn't stand to come home anymore, it broke my heart. I have no one and no where to go. You are my everything. I tried to give you a baby, but I failed at that too. I will now go to be with our baby girl."

Yours always,
Cynthia your devoted wife

Tears streamed my eyes. When I heard the door bell I ran out of my father's room and down the stairs. I blindly opened the door. I ran back up stairs and the police and ambulance followed. They took pictures of the scene. They asked me if there had been a note. I showed them the note. They took Cynthia and it away. Through sweat and tears I cleaned up the bathroom and tried to dry what I could of the bathroom floor and rugs. When my father came home I did not greet him at the door, nor was his slippers there. When he came into his room there was no Cynthia. The next room that he went to was mine. I was waiting for this meeting. He asked where Cynthia was. I told him that she had went to hell to prepare a way for him. He looked at me with a puzzled look. I had written the note over, drawing the exact words from my memory. I handed it to him. He took it and while still in my doorway read it. For a second I thought I saw emotion, but then he just walked away."

"What went through your mind then?"

Monic thought about the question.

"I was angry with him for making another substitution go away."

"I don't understand."

"She took my place. I didn't have to be the wife anymore.

A week later my father brought Carry home. She was fifteen. She seemed so innocent. I felt sorry for her. I was cordial. Again I filled her in on her duties. She carried them out well. She was exceptionally clean. She was a pretty girl, nice shape. She looked younger than her fifteen years. When my father came home everything went as always except I no longer ate dinner with my father and his child mistress.

At night I would turn my radio up to block out the sounds of my father and his new mistress.

Three months went by and I had come home early from school. We had half a day. Carry was in the den watching music videos. I thought, if she had gone to my school we might have been friends. I spoke and she spoke back. She went for the remote. I told her that she could leave it on. I asked her how did she meet my father. She said that she met him a year ago outside of the skating rink. I asked her how is it that her parents let her come to live here. She told me that she was homeless. That my father had rescued her. She said that her parents were drug addicts, they moved around a lot. The night that she met my father she was begging for money to help her parents get drugs. She said that he had given her money in return for sex. She further explained that night she fell in love with him. She explained that he had been so gentle. She had told him that she was a virgin. She was surprised that her first time would feel so good. She said that my father was her knight, that her dreams were answered when she met him. She went on to say that every night he holds her and make sweat love to her. Carry said, "I love your father. I know that I'm young, but I would have a far worst life if he had not come along.

Although I could appreciate her circumstances I didn't think that she should be with my father. I asked her did she have any other family. She didn't. I asked her didn't she feel awkward being with a man his age and taking care of his house. She said that she liked the fact that he knew what he was doing in bed and knew how to please her. She also liked being his wife, although they weren't officially married.

CHAPTER 5

Rebellion Years

I believe at sixteen years old I came into my own. Maybe they call it my rebellion stage. I didn't have meals with my father any more. I spoke to him because that had been bread in me, but I came and went as I pleased. I still went to the skating rink on Saturdays and on Fridays I hung out at the club for teens. I met this guy named Joseph. He was real nice. We dated for a few weeks. He was eighteen. He had a Camaro.

On our fifth date we went to a drive-in-movie. We started out watching the movie, then Joseph put his arm around my shoulders. He moved me closer to him. He took the hand that was around my shoulders and turned my face towards his. He kissed me. I tried to play hard to get. So after the kiss I turned my head and began watching the movie again. He turned my head and kissed me again. This time the kiss was longer. We kissed for a while and then he said lets get in the back seat, so we can get comfortable.

We got in the back seat. Again I pretended to be interested in the movie. Joseph pulled me to him and kissed me. He eased me down and laid on top of me. We kissed for the rest of the movie. After the movie had been off a while I stopped kissing him. I lied and told him that I had to get home. He didn't argue. He drove me home. He tried to kiss me and I told him not in front of my house. Although my father had a wife and I was older than what he liked I still had fear if he knew that I was having sex he would change.

For our next date Joseph took me to the movies again. This time we sat in the back as soon as we parked. When the movie began Joseph asked for a kiss. I kissed him. It was a long sensuous kiss. I knew that he was going to try to have sex with me. I continued to kiss him and let him touch me, but I didn't feel anything. Eventually I stopped him. I told him that I was saving myself. He looked at me and asked why. That was the last time that we went out......

I began hanging out at the teen club again. I met a couple of guys, but I wasn't interested. One Friday I met this guy by the name of Thomas at the teen club. He was nineteen. He asked me to dance. We danced to two songs. Then he asked me if we could go somewhere it was quiet. I followed him outside. He smoothed his hand over my face. He told me that I was so pretty. I blushed. He asked me if he could kiss me. I said yes. He lightly kissed me. The kiss was very short. He said you have soft lips. He kissed me again. I was shocked that I felt tingles. Other than kissing me, we did not touch. He stopped kissing me and asked me would I like to sit in his car. We got into his car. His front seat was huge and the gears were in the steering wheel. He asked me if he could kiss me again. I shook my head in approval. He kissed me. He began to touch me. I wanted to say no, but I liked it. He eased me under him. We continued to kiss. After we had kissed and he aroused all of my senses he asked me if I was on the pill. I told him no. He told me that he didn't have a condom. I told him that it was alright. He began to kiss me again. As our passion rose he made himself one with me. We moved in unison until our pleasure exploited. He kissed me slowly. He said, "That was nice. I hope we can do this again."

It was getting late. I told him that I had to get home. He drove me home. He asked me for my number. I gave it to him. When I went to get out of the car he pulled my arm. I looked back. He moved towards me and quickly kissed me on the lips. I got out of the car and headed into my house. I went upstairs to my room. It was late and the house was quiet. I looked out of my room window. I watched as Thomas pulled off. I laid in my bed and thought about what we had just done. I held my body. I smiled as I thought of Thomas touching me. He was so gentle and seemed to care about me. I thought that I was foolish because how can this man care about me and we had just met. But it did seem so. I felt something for him. It was strange. I had never felt this way before. I drifted off to sleep thinking of this new man in my life.

The next day Thomas called me. He told me that I sounded surprised. I confessed that I was surprised and pleased to hear from him. He called me everyday. I began to look forward to his calls....

Months went by and we began to date. We were

hot and heavy for a few months. For a while it was just Thomas and I being together.

One day Lori called me and asked me to go with her and some others out. I decided to take her up on her offer. I went to the skating rink with the girls. We skated around the room and danced sometime on ring side. I met Bobby that night. We talked throughout the night. He and I had a lot in common. He asked for my phone number. I gave it to him.

When the night was over Bobby asked when would be a good time to call. I gave him times when I didn't expect Thomas to call.

I was still a honors student. I was working on getting a full scholarship and wanted to go away to college. I tried to divide my time up with my best friend, Thomas and Bobby. I talked to Lori on the phone and sometimes we would go to the movies or to the skating rink. I only went to the teen club with Thomas and skating rink with Bobby. Thomas and I had sex in his car at least three times a week.

After I met Bobby and we got close I began sneaking Bobby up to my room. His parents were always home, he didn't have a car and Carry was the only one at my house until my father came home at seven. Then he and Carry went upstairs by nine and they were doing their own thing.

When I first started sneaking Bobby up to my room it was after school and we would study. We sometimes went to the library, but we couldn't really talk there. He was attending community college. He didn't want to bring a girl home because his parents would accuse him of not being serious about school so I brought him home with me. No one ever knew he was there......

After five months of bringing him over after school, twice a week things got serious. I remember the first time with him. He met me after I got out of school. When I got home I opened the door, checked to see where Carry was and then brought Bobby in. We went upstairs. I locked my door. We studied a while. After an hour of studying Bobby asked me for a kiss. This would be our first kiss. I didn't respond right away. I wondered if I would be turned off if he wasn't a good kisser. I guess he thought that I was rejecting him, because he went back to reading his book. I moved the book. He looked up at me. I said, I didn't say no. He moved in closer. As our lips met our eyes closed. We kissed a few minutes and then he pulled away. He said I think that's enough. I don't want to start anything. I asked him why not. I wanted to kiss him again. He explained that he didn't want something to happen and we get caught. I assured him that wouldn't happen. He explained that he was referring to me getting pregnant. I assured him that if we decided to have sex I was taken care of. He told me that he didn't want to rush into anything. I told him that we didn't have to do anything other than kiss. I remembered my first time experiencing pleasure without taking any of my clothes off.

I took the first step. I kissed him. We were still sitting at my desk. I turned my chair to face his so we could be closer. He tried to pull me to him, but the chairs made this difficult. I eased out of my chair, still kissing him, I sat on his lap. As the kiss became more intense he began touching my breast. Then he moved his hand down to my pants. He caressed my body. As things steamed up he stopped. He asked if we could move to the bed. I got up, took him by the hand and walked over to the bed. I layed down on the bed. It was 9:30 by then, so I knew that my father and Carry was in their room. He began to kiss me again. He kissed me other places as well. We still had our clothes on. I didn't think that he was ready for sex so I didn't try to take my clothes off. I let him do what he was comfortable with. That was kissing and caressing me. He didn't even try to get on top of me. After a while he stopped himself and said that he had to go. I understood, but I was so aroused and I needed relief.

After he left I called Thomas. He was available and said that he would come to pick me up. I just told him that I wanted to see him. Within an half hour I went outside and Thomas was there. I got into his car. I kissed him lightly. This wasn't our usual night so he wasn't aware that I wanted to have sex. We drove around at first, just talking about the people on the street and his job and me at school. We ended up at a deserted area. He leaned over and kissed me. He touched my breast and then unbuttoned my pants. He caressed me as we kissed. Soon we were laying down, he on top of me and moving erotically. When we couldn't stand being apart we became one. I had longed for this feeling. We layed there in each others arms. He kissed me. After we had laid there a little while I said I have to get back home because I had school in the morning. He began to move on top of me again. He kissed me and my body responded. It was 2 a.m. when I returned home.

The next night was our usual night and he wanted to see me. After getting up to my room my phone rang. It was Bobby. He apologized for leaving me like he did. He said that he just wanted to be ready, for both of us to be ready. He said that he wanted our first encounter to be special. I told him that it was ok. He blew a kiss through the phone and said good night.

The next day was Friday. Thomas and I went to the club. We danced all night. When the club closed we went to Thomas' car. He drove to a secluded place. He turned off the car leaned the seat back and then placed his arm around my shoulders. He pulled me close to him and then kissed me. He began to touch my breast. Once the kiss became fiery he moved me back, laying me down. He laid on top of me. We kissed for a while. He rotated his body about me. We continued to kiss and then he began to take off my clothes. He caressed my body until I couldn't stand to be apart from him. He must have sensed this because he joined me in an erotic movement. He pulled his pants down and we became one. We kissed and moved together until our bodies exploited into ecstasy. We laid there for a few minutes. Once we had recovered from our love making he took me home.

When I got home and went into my room the phone was ringing. I answered it. It was Bobby. He told me that he couldn't get me off his mind. He said that all he's been able to think about was the last time that we were together. He wanted to know what I was doing the next weekend. I told him that I was available. I figured I would cancel my usual night out with Thomas. I was curious about Bobby. Our last or should I say only encounter made me wonder about his skills.

By Thursday I was so excited. Bobby had made a reservation for us to spend Friday and Saturday night together. Thursday Thomas and I hung out. We drove around and then parked in our usual spot. He made his usual moves and I responded, but this time I thought of Bobby. After I pulled my clothes up I asked Thomas to take me home. He asked me was everything ok. I told him it was. I liked Thomas. He was a lot of fun and love making was great. He knew what he was doing and he made sure that I always felt good and left satisfied. I didn't mean to seem distant and Thomas deserved more, but Bobby was on my mind. It wasn't just the thought of Bobby himself, it was the fact that he took the time to make things romantic.

The next day I watched the clock in school. Bobby said that he was going to meet me after school, so I put some clothes in my pocket book and brought it to school with me. I told my father that I was staying over a friend's house for the weekend. I told Thomas not to call me because I was going away for the weekend. He assumed I was going with my father and his new wife (girlfriend). I let him believe that.

When school was over I rushed out. I looked around, but didn't see Bobby. I got concerned; then this car that was parked in front of the school beeped his horn. I peered inside. It was Bobby. He got out of the car and ran around to the passenger's side and opened the door for me. I got in. When he got in the car he reached over and kissed me. I asked him whose car it was. He told me it was his father's. We drove to the hotel. He asked me if I was hungry. I told him a little, so he ordered pizza. We ate and watched television. He told me that he had gotten accepted at Lincoln University in Pennsylvania. He was so happy. I hugged him. I was excited for him. He said he was leaving in January. He told me that he would miss me. I told him that I would miss him too and he could write me. He said that he would. We talked for hours. With Bobby we had an intellectual relationship. Although there was an obvious physical attraction he never acted on it. After a while we got quiet. I had been sitting up on the bed and Bobby was sitting in the window seal. It had gotten late so I laid down. Bobby came over and got in the bed next to me. He put his arm around my back and we fell asleep.

At one in the morning I woke up to Bobby kissing the back of my neck. When he realized that I was awake he turned me over onto my back. He kissed me on my chest and then he kissed me on my lips. I laid still, not even moving my arms. He unbuttoned my blouse, revealing my bra. He put his hand inside my bra and caressed my breast. I continued to lay still. He kissed me again while continuing to caress my breast. It was hard just laying there, but I just wanted him to make me feel good. I returned his kiss. He was such a good kisser. He then unbuttoned and unzipped my pants. He stopped kissing me only long enough to remove my pants. Bobby smoothed his hand over my body. I shivered. He asked me if I was I cold. I told him no. He went to the head of the bed and pulled the covers back. I got under the covers. He pulled them back off of me. He smoothed his hand over my entire body saying that my skin was so soft. He kissed me all over and ran his tong all over my body sending shivers throughout it. My body tensed and moved uncontrollably. He took pleasure in seeing this. He kissed me again. He continued to touch my body, arousing me again. He climbed on top of me and we began to move together. He whispered my name and we became one. We moved in unison until our bodies erupted with pleasure. We held onto each other and soon drifted off to sleep.

The next day when we awakened we went down to the hotel restaurant and ate lunch. We then went swimming. We hung out at the indoor pool. We swam and played in the pool. We got some snacks and went back to our room. Bobby ordered a movie on the television. It was a comedy. We laughed and ate our snacks. When the movie was over Bobby asked me if he could make love to me again. I answered him by taking off my clothes. For the rest of our stay we made love.

We woke up at 10 the next morning. We dressed and checked out. Bobby drove me home. He parked in front of my house. He kissed me with such passion that I could barely breathe. He told me that he loved me. I looked at him, not believing what I had heard. He said Monic I am in love with you. My heart went out to him, knowing how I felt when I told Carlos. I kissed him and said that I loved him too. Just as I got out of the car he took my hand. I looked back and smiled. He told me he would call me. I went into my house and went up to my room. I laid on my bed and thought of my weekend with Bobby. Just thinking about it made my body react. That night Thomas called me. He asked about my weekend. I said with such passion that it was wonderful that he questioned if I had gone with my father. I told him no. He got quiet. I didn't know what to say. I liked Thomas, but after my weekend with Bobby and what he said to me confused me. I didn't want to stop seeing Thomas, but I didn't want to be unfaithful to Bobby. After our silence I told Thomas that it wasn't anything he needed to worry about. This seemed to cheer him up and he was back to his usual cheery self. We talked throughout the night, falling asleep on the phone.

The next morning I said bye to Thomas and got ready for school. I tried to stay away from Thomas, not wanting to do anything with him, because of Bobby. Instead I talked on the phone with Thomas.

A week went past and I hadn't heard from Bobby. I wondered if my saying that I loved him scared him off. Then I thought, he said it first.

Another week went by and I still hadn't heard from Bobby. I had stayed away from Thomas for two weeks. I refused to call Bobby.

It was three weeks since my weekend with Bobby. I was feeling lonely. Since I had met Thomas I had not gone without having sex in more than a couple of days. I was craving to be touched, but I was holding out for Bobby.....

By Friday I was becoming weak. Thomas had called and said that he missed me. He wanted us to go out. I told him that I was taking a break, to be patient. He was..... Saturday came and Bobby called. He apologized for not calling before then. I told him not to worry about it. He asked me to meet him at the skating rink. I told him that I'd be there. All day I was anxious.....

When I saw him I quickly walked over to him. He didn't try to kiss or hug me. We sat down. He told me that he meant what he said, but he didn't want any distractions. He said that it would be too many years to ask me to wait and I was too young to give up my youth. He said that he wouldn't do that to me. He said that tonight would be the last time we spent together because he had to get ready for school. I didn't bother to tell him that it was my birthday. I accepted his decision and didn't feel any ill will for him. You see I had gotten accustom to being dumped after I confess my feelings. Again I had told a guy how I felt and lost him. I told him that I didn't feel well and that I needed to go home. Bobby saw me home. I kissed him and knew it would be my last time. I went into the house and up to my room. I laid across my bed and began to cry. My phone rang. I picked it up. I tried not to sound upset. It was Thomas. He heard sadness in my voice. He asked me what was wrong. Well I couldn't tell him the truth, so I just said that it was my birthday and no one had said anything. He said I'm sorry I forgot, "Happy Birthday." He asked me if I wanted to do something. I said I didn't know. He said look I'm going to come to get you and we're going to spend your birthday together. He said get dressed. I dressed and went downstairs. Thomas was waiting. I got into his car. He drove to the teen club. We danced all night.

After the club closed Thomas drove me to a hotel. We went up to our room. I couldn't believe that he had gotten a room for us. We entered the room. I turned on the television. I turned the channels to see what was on. A music video came on. Thomas took me by the hand and started dancing. He danced up on me. Then he held me from behind and kissed my neck. We continued to move to the music. He turned me around and kissed me on the lips. I had missed being held. I put my arms around his neck. He had his hands around my waist. He pulled me to his body and we began to kiss. We stood there kissing a while. I could tell he was getting aroused. He moved his hand to the top of my behind and pulled me closer. I could feel his hardness against my body. He began backing me towards the bed. He said I missed you, I missed this. I told him me too. He laid me onto the bed and then laid beside me. He unbuttoned my blouse. I laid there. I actually liked for the guys to undress me. After unbuttoning my blouse he opened it and looked at my breast. He kissed my breast; then he caressed them. He unsnapped my bra and removed it as well. He cupped my breast and teased each one with his tongue and teeth. I held the back of his head. He moved his hands down to my pants and unfastened them. I eased up for him to take them off. He kissed my lower stomach as he removed my pants. He said nice. I lay there with nothing on except my panties. He smoothed his hand over them making my temperature rise. He removed his clothes. This was the first time that I really saw his body, because we were always in his car. His muscles were well defined. When he laid next to me I smoothed my hand over his chest. He said oh you like that. I did but I didn't tell him. He kissed my neck. Just then I remembered that last time that I had been in the hotel and the conversation that I had with Bobby. I got sad and laid my head on Thomas' chest. He didn't say anything, he just put his arms around me and held me. Although tears filled my eyes I wouldn't cry. He moved my head up and kissed my eyes. His lips wet from my tears, I kissed them. I asked him to hold me. He held me and caressed my back. We fell asleep.

A few hours later I woke up. Thomas was still holding me. I caressed his chest and then kissed him. After a few minutes he awakened and returned my kiss. He pulled me on top of him. I could feel his arousal. He held me tight. After some time kissing and moving together we became one. I didn't realize how much I had missed this feeling, until Thomas and I embraced. We hung onto each other as to capture that moment and keep it forever. As if he was trying to love away my hurt Thomas began to kiss me. He held me tight and with firm hands touched parts of my body arousing every part he touched. He rolled me over onto my back. He kissed me from head to toe. We became one again. We kissed and moved slowly as to savor every moment and every feeling. Our movements brought us to heights we had not felt before. Thomas kissed me with uncontrolled trembling. Thomas remained on top of me. Neither one of us wanted to move. As our bodies began to relax Thomas whispered I love you. I held him tighter to reassure him that I cared, but I was afraid to say the words. I did love Thomas. We had been together for a while and he had been there for me through some difficult times. I didn't want to lose him. We fell asleep, just the way we were. We awakened at ten the next morning. The passion was still there. We finally left at twelve in the afternoon. We were quite throughout the ride. Thomas had placed his arm around my shoulders. I sat as close as I could without being on his lap. He caressed my arm. I laid my head on his chest and it felt so good. When he pulled up to my house, for the first time I didn't want to leave him. I didn't want this feeling to end. We sat there for a while. As if we both realized it, I took my head off his shoulder. He took the hand that had been caressing my shoulder, moved my face towards him and kissed me passionately. He stopped and said you better go. I hope your birthday turned out better than it started. I gave him a light kiss, said it had and thanked him.

Thomas and I began to date exclusively. I didn't look at any other guy.....

Graduation was coming up. I was so excited. I had gotten accepted with a full scholarship to several colleges. I only applied to colleges that were away. Thomas was happy for me, but he hated the fact that I wanted to go away. I told Thomas that I had wanted to go away from the time my mother got sick and died and that I had not thought of anything else until now. I had fallen in love with Thomas. I still had not confessed this to him. Thomas and I spent as much time together as possible.

I was given three tickets for my graduation ceremony. I gave Thomas a ticket to my graduation. At this point I didn't care that my father knew I had a boyfriend. I was seventeen now and could take care of myself, besides I was too old for my husband now. I also gave a ticket to my father and Carry. They were the only family that I had.

The day of graduation I had to go to school for half a day. Thomas met me after school. He drove me home. He told me that he would pick me up when I was ready.....

He came back two hours later. I had to be at the graduation early. My father and Carry were coming later.

Thomas sat and watched our graduation rehearsal. We got set up and it was time for my big moment. As they called my name I got up. The first person I saw was Thomas. He was clapping and whistling. Then I saw my father and Carry. They were clapping. For that brief moment I was happy and proud that I had people who cared. I collected my diploma and sat back down.

After the ceremony was over I met my boyfriend and family outside. I introduced Thomas to Carry and then my father. They shook hands. I told my father that I was going away for the weekend. He looked at me. I told him that a lot of the students were going away to celebrate graduation weekend. My father told me that he had something for me when I return home. Thomas and I left....

We had rented a cabin for the weekend. As we drove to the cabin Thomas asked how old Carry was. I was embarrassed so I lied. I told him that she looks younger than she was. I didn't tell him her age. Thomas said that he couldn't believe how young my father's girlfriend was. I told him that I didn't want to talk about it. He apologized for upsetting me. I told him not to worry about it.

When we got to the cabin it was late. We changed out of our graduation clothes and into lounging clothes. We ordered take-out because it was so late. When the take-out came we ate and talked about our relationship. Thomas said that he didn't expect me to not talk to other guys when I go away. I argued that I would be faithful. He told me that he knew that I would be away for a while and I may be attracted to someone else and he wouldn't hold it against me. I told him that I would see him every holiday and when I had breaks. Then I told him that I didn't want to talk about it any more. The rest of the night we talked of lighter things.

The next day we went down to the beach. He won me a few stuffed animals. We played in the water and ate funnel cakes and candy apples. We took cheese steaks and French fries back to the cabin. We made love and made promises to each other.....

When the weekend was over I returned home. I went to my room. On the bed was a card. I opened it and a pair of car keys fell out.

The letter said:

"I wanted to give you these in person, but you had plans. Congratulations baby and enjoy your new BMW. Oh look in the glove compartment for the registration and insurance. "

Daddy loves you.

I ran outside. I couldn't believe that I didn't see the car in front of the house. I ran to it and opened the door. I sat in it, looked around and smoothed my hand over the seats. I turned the car on. I screamed with joy. I couldn't believe that I had a new car and not just a new car, a BMW. I pulled off and drove through the city. I drove back home and parked my car. I turned it off and sat in it for an hour. I finally went back to my room. I called Thomas. He had been asleep. I told him I was sorry for waking him, but I had to tell someone and he was the only one I could think to call. I told him about the car. He was excited for me…..

The next morning I left a note on my father's door thanking him for the car.

For the rest of the summer Thomas and I spent every waking moment together. He helped me get things together for college. As time got closer to me going away I began getting sad. While couldn't wait to get out of that house, I knew I was leaving everything that I knew, even if it was bad. I also dreaded leaving Thomas. We had become so close.

The week before I was to leave Thomas decided that he would drive me to my school. He would drive my car and catch the train back. This made me happy, not only that I would have transportation, but I would get to spend more time with Thomas and he would know where I was if he decided to visit me. I hoped that he would want to come back.

The day we got ready to leave I wished Carry well and said goodbye to my father. He gave me money and a credit card. He told me to call if I needed anything. I thought to myself "I was finally leaving." I was partly happy, but there was sadness too. I was leaving the only home that I'd ever known. As we drove away I rested my head on Thomas' shoulder and tears streamed my eyes. Thomas put his arm around my shoulder. I couldn't believe that I was actually sad......

CHAPTER 6

College Life

As Thomas drove I took in the scenery. I had never really been too far from my home. The scenery was beautiful. I pretended Thomas and I were moving away together. I smiled thinking how it was just he and I. I drifted off to sleep a few times and woke up once when we stopped to fill up. We walked around the welcome center and I thought of purchasing some mementos, and then I thought who would I share them with. We got on our way again. I was driving. Thomas drifted off to sleep. I glanced at him a few times. He was so handsome. I smoothed my hand over his face. I did it lightly, not wanting to wake him. I wanted him to get his rest.....

Well I made it to school. Thomas stayed the weekend to rest. It was nice being with him away from home. It was like we had gone away on vacation. We stayed in. We shut the world out. I didn't want to share him with anyone, even though we didn't know anyone. When Thomas got ready to leave it felt strange. I dropped him at the train station. I stayed until the train was out of site. I got into my car and drove off. My eyes became watery. I wiped them and continued driving. When I got back to my apartment I became afraid. I had never been by myself before and with Thomas still traveling home I couldn't call him. I laid in bed wondering if I had made a mistake. Then I thought how all of my life I had wanted to be far away from the hell that I lived in. But to be true to myself, I couldn't believe I even thought of it, I felt safe there. Everything was taken care of. Those people were the only family that I knew, or ever had. I wondered if I would be able to make it alone in life......

Monday morning I got up, dressed and headed out into my new world. I managed to find my way around the campus. I went to get my schedule and then purchased my books. On my way back to my apartment I stopped and got something to eat. It felt different eating at my own table. I only ate a little of it, because I lost my appetite. I decided to go to bed early.

Tuesday I got up. I didn't bother to eat. I decided to look through my books. I went to bed early anticipating my classes.

Wednesday I got up, dressed and drove to the campus. I found my classes well enough. Thinking about where I was I became excited. I loved school. I knew it would take me away from my problems.

After returning to my apartment Thomas called me. It was good hearing from him and I longed to feel his touch. He told me that he would come back in two weeks to spend the weekend with me. I looked forward to that. I carried on with attending my classes and getting to know my way around.

The weeks went by quickly. When it was time to pick Thomas up I got into my car and headed to the train station. I arrived there before the train came in. I sat on an empty bench. As the train approached I stood up. I stayed there frozen until it had come and had stopped in front of me. I excitedly stood there anticipating seeing Thomas. When he stepped off of the train I stood there not being able to move. Thomas smiled when he saw me and quickly descended the train. He was carrying a duffle bag and rushed over to me. I managed to move my feet and met him half way. We embraced as if we had not seen each other in years. I held him tightly, not ever wanting to let him go. He joked and said oh I guess you missed me. I said maybe a little. I told Thomas where I was parked. We walked arm in arm to my car. I opened the doors. Thomas placed his bag in the back seat. We got into the car. Thomas placed his hand on the back of my chair and caressed my shoulders. We headed back to my place. I told him that there was a party Saturday and asked him if he wanted to go. He said yeah. We stayed inside and ordered Chinese, which taste a little different. We caught up for two weeks.

The next morning we went out to breakfast. After breakfast I gave him a tour of the campus. Afterwards we drove around the city. All the while he had his hand behind my neck, caressing it. It felt so good. It was a familiar touch. I got sad, because I knew he would be leaving on Sunday. Then I stopped myself. I wanted to enjoy this time with Thomas. I knew soon enough he would be gone and I would have plenty of time to be lonely and sad. We went back to my place. We laid down and held each other. We soon fell asleep.

When we woke up we ate dinner and then dressed for the party. We drove back to the campus. We danced to every song. Towards the end of the party they played an old slow song by the Whispers. Thomas held me tight and we danced as if no one was around. I could feel that Thomas had missed me. The feel was almost like desperation. He kissed me with such intensity it made my head whirl. He then whispered in my ear, can we leave. I felt the same way and the party was about over any way. As I droved back to my place Thomas kissed my neck and caressed my thighs. When we got back to my place we held onto each other and Thomas kissed me as we walked up to my place. We went into my apartment. We stumbled as we kissed and undressed each other. I never thought that I could feel what I did that night. As tears rolled down my eyes, we made love until the sun came up.

Sunday morning came and it was time for Thomas to leave. We reluctantly got up. We went to a nearby restaurant and had breakfast. I was too sad to be hungry, but I tried to eat a little because I didn't want to waist the food. I tried not to appear sad. After we left the restaurant we got into my car and started out for the train station. Tears drenched my eyes as I drove to the train station. Thomas tried to wipe them away. When we got to the station I parked and waited with him. As the train neared the station Thomas held me tight around the waist and kissed me passionately. I held him tight, not wanting to let him go, but I knew he had to. When he got on the train I stood there watching the train, not being able to move until it had move out of sight....

Thomas tried to come out to see me every other

weekend. He made sure he came for my birthday. We partied the entire weekend. After that weekend Thomas stopped coming every two weeks and began coming once a month. I made friends and went out with them on the weekends that he wasn't due to come. Although I missed him I enjoyed hanging out with the girls. Thomas and I talked twice a week. I found the classes to be interesting and some to be challenging, but I kept my 4.0 average.

When winter break came I decided not to go home. I wrote and told my father. I didn't want to go back there. Thomas was disappointed. I tried to get him to come out and spend it with me. He said that there weren't any trains or buses and he didn't want to drive the distance at such a late time and couldn't get the time off. I accepted his decision, but knew things were changing. We talked during my break when Thomas was off. I was very lonely, but I didn't ever want to go back to that house. This was the first time that I had ever felt so lonely, because I couldn't tell Thomas my secret. I couldn't tell anyone...

After that break Thomas became more distant. He stopped calling as much and months went by without him coming to see me.

When summer came I had gotten a job. I asked Thomas to come down on his vacation. He expressed that maybe we should step back. Although I knew this was coming it was still devastating. He thought that I had made a new life here and it didn't include him. I tried to explain that it wasn't that I didn't want to see him. It was that for the first time I felt a peace. I had no worries and didn't have to see my father's sickness. I was afraid to tell Thomas. I was afraid of what he would think of me. I accepted his decision, told him that I would always love him and said goodbye.

After the breakup with Thomas I studied even more, determined that I would be successful at one thing in my life. I decided to write my father. I told him that I would not be returning and I thanked him for giving me somewhere to live when my mother died. I told him that I hoped that he would do right by Carry and said goodbye.

"Did he write back?"

"No and I was fine with that. Although I had a full scholarship and my father was sending me money I got a job. I wanted to make sure that if he ever stopped sending me money I would be able to live comfortably. I was happy that my father never tried to change my mind. Other than paying the credit card that he gave me and sending me a check once a month I never heard from him.

I doubled up on my courses. I even managed to pay for two classes each Summer.

My third year I accepted an invitation by friends to go to a party. I dressed and met them there. I sat around most of the night. I felt out of place. It had been the first party since Thomas and I had broken up. A couple of guys asked me to dance, but I declined. I didn't want to get involved again. As the time wore down a young man sat down beside me. He spoke, but very casual. I returned his greeting. Out of nowhere he struck up a conversation. I was surprised that I was actually enjoying the conversation. We talked until the end of the party. When everyone was leaving he said, "By the way my name is Charles." I told him my name and said it was nice to talk with him. He walked me to my car. We said good night.

I returned to my apartment. I took the chance and called my high school friend Lori. She had stayed home and gone to a school in state. I was happy that she was still awake. I told her what had been going on in my life and she told me about her life. We talked for hours.....

Before we got off the phone she told me that she had seen Thomas. My heart sunk. I still missed him. She said that he was doing well. He was in College. I was happy for him. I thanked her for the update and told her to stay in touch. I told her to tell him hi for me, if she was to run into him again.

After hanging the phone up I laid there and reminisced about the times that I spent with Thomas. I fell asleep wishing that I was still with him.

The next day I got up and went to church. I went early and sat there praying to God to help me be content with my life. During service I was thankful for going.

After leaving church I drove around the city. I pulled over and parked when I saw a museum. I went inside and looked around. I got on the elevator to go up to the second level. Inside the elevator was Charles. He smiled and said hi. I returned his greeting. He joked, asking me if I was following him. We both laughed. For a minute I thought of Carlos. Carlos had a nice personality that drew you into him. Charles asked me if I was alone. I told him that I was. He asked if he could join me in my tour of the museum. I said if he'd like.

As we toured Charles was very charming. He actually knew a lot about art. I was enjoying myself. After the tour he asked me if I had any plans for lunch. I told him no.

He invited me out to lunch. We drove separate cars. He talked all during lunch. We were there for two hours. I hated it when lunch was over. He walked me to my car, Charles thanked me for the day and then I drove off. As I drove back to my apartment I thought about the two encounters with Charles. I thought how nice it was talking with him. I missed having someone in my life.

Monday I got up and went to class. When I arrived there I sat in my usual seat. I was early so I looked over my notes. Someone came up behind me and tapped me on the shoulder. I looked up. I was taken aback. It was Charles. I asked him what he was doing there. He told me that he was in this class. I couldn't believe it. All semester this charming man had been in my class and I never noticed. He showed me where he sat.

After class we sat under a tree and talked about the class. He asked me if I had any more classes today. I told him that was it for the day. He told me that he had one more class and no plans for the night. He said that he would like to see me later. I tried not to show that I was thrilled that I would have someone to talk to tonight. I accepted his invitation. He told me that he knew a quiet restaurant where they had a live band, good food and where we could get to know each other. He asked if I wanted to be picked up or meet him. I told him that he could pick me up. I was lonely, enjoyed his company and didn't want to drive home alone later......

He came to pick me up at four o'clock. He beeped the horn, I came out of the house and got into his car. He drove for an half hour. During that time he asked me if I was from here. He asked if I had a boyfriend back home or in the area. I told him that I was from Jersey and didn't have a boyfriend anywhere. He said good. I looked at him curious, but did not reply. Soon we pulled up to the restaurant. Charles parked the car and we went into the restaurant. We sat at a table near the band. As the band played we ate our meal and talked. Charles told me about himself. I talked about my life since I had been in college. I told him that my past was boring. After we had finished eating Charles asked me if I'd like to dance. I got up and we danced slow to a couple of songs. He was a good dancer. I liked the way that he held me.

It was late when we left the restaurant. When we pulled up to my door Charles turned off the engine. We talked for an hour. He then told me that he had a good time and would like to see me again. I told him that I would like that as well......

Charles and I began to study together and spend our free days together. I was working at the hospital three days a week and interning two days a week. Charles was a good student, very focused and helped me with my studying. It was nice having someone to study with.

Six months later Charles and I began to date. Whenever I or he wasn't in class or working we were together. I enjoyed my time with Charles. He wasn't Thomas. He was different and I liked the time that we spent together. We graduated together. My father came to my graduation. I was cordial and introduced him to Charles. As usual Charles was charming. We had dinner with my father. I asked my father about Carry. He told me that she was eight months pregnant and hated missing my graduation. I told my father to tell Carry congratulations. Deep down I was sad for her and hoped that she would have a son. My father paid for dinner. We all left the restaurant and headed to our cars. I said goodbye to my father and he drove off. Charles drove me home. Once we arrived outside of my house Charles parked the car and we remained in it. Charles asked me about my father. I told him that we just weren't close. He accepted my explanation.

For the first time he told me that he didn't want the night to end. I looked at him and asked him what he wanted to do. He reached over and drew me close to him. He kissed me. Before we had lightly kissed and said good night. This kiss was passionate. I told him that we could continue our conversation in my apartment.

When we entered the apartment I turned some music on and asked if he was thirsty. He walked over to me and placed his hands on my waist. He drew me close and kissed me. I placed my arms around his shoulders. We stood there and kissed. He stopped and asked me if he could make love to me. For the first time I was hesitant. I had not had intercourse for over two years and I had not planned to get into anything serious again. Charles noticed my hesitation and released my waist. We sat down in the living room. I explained to him that I had not been out with anyone in over two years. I told him that my hesitation was not a rejection, that I was kind of nervous.

He stood up. He held his hand out to me. I took it. Slow music was playing. He and I began to slow dance. As we danced Charles pulled me closer to his body. He placed his hands at the tip of my behind. As the soft music continued we danced. He bent his head and we began to kiss. He moved down to my neck. As he kissed my neck, we continued to dance. He started to unbutton my blouse.

I did not try to stop him. When it was unbuttoned he pulled it out of my pants and took it off. He threw it on the chair. We continued to sway to the music. Charles cupped my breast and then bent down and kissed them. He took his hands off of me just a few minutes to take off his shirt. After placing his shirt on the chair he removed my pants, leaving me in my bra and panties. Charles took me into his arms again and we swayed to the music. He took one of my hands in his and the other caressed my back. He softly and with a smooth touch ran his hand down the sensitive part of my back. Charles must have felt me shiver because he picked me up and carried me into my bedroom. He laid me onto the bed. His pants remained on. He took his shoes off. As he removed my shoes from my feet he kissed each one. Charles ran his hand down my bare legs. I had forgotten what this felt like. He kissed, caressed and teased my body. My body trembled under his touch. He stopped and took off his pants. After removing his pants he sat next to me. He eased me up and unsnapped my bra. He touched my breast with such a gentle touch that without a response from my body I would have not known he touched them. I moaned. He did not stop. His touch was maddening. Although I longed for him I allowed him to continue his seduction. He touched my lips and then kissed them. He paused for just long enough to remove his boxers, exposing his arousal. He began kissing me again. As we kissed he continued to touch my body. My body called to him. He pulled me on top of him and we became one. We made love throughout the night. Our bodies took over and we no longer controlled our thoughts. We made love until our bodies were satisfied. We held onto each other, not speaking. We fell asleep laying together as one.

The next morning I awakened first. I smoothed my hand over his body. It felt so good to wake up in Charles arms. I remembered the times that I had awakened in Thomas' arms. I hadn't realized how much I missed this feeling. I laid there and nestled my head in his chest. I soon fell back to sleep. When I awakened again Charles was kissing me. I returned his kiss. He stopped kissing me and asked if I was hungry. I told him that I could eat something. We dressed and went to IHOP. As we ate he asked me if I enjoyed the night. I told him I had. He asked me what my plans were for the future. I told him that I was continuing school; that I had signed up to go to the graduate program and then going to get my doctorates so I can be a Psychiatrist. He informed me that he was returning home to New York and going to grad school there.

He asked me to come with him. I was flattered, but I had my life planned out at least until I was finished school and I didn't want to change them. I was tempted. It was nice having someone to spend time with and this last event made me want to follow him. I had lost several guys due to my ideas, but I couldn't start changing my plans now. They were about me, who I am and I had to stick to them no matter what the cost. Charles remained the rest of the Summer. He showed me so many wonderful things. We went to several different nearby states, taking in their historical sites, eating at fancy restaurants, visiting beaches and the nights were wonderful.

At the end of August, Charles had packed up and came to my apartment. He tried to get me to change my mind. As I watched his car drive away I for a brief moment, I panic and thought of taking him up on his offer. Then I came back to my senses and I went into my empty apartment. I laid in my bed clutching my pillow all night and wondering if I had made a mistake. Charles was a great guy. I evaluated my life. I thought about every relationship that I had and what happened in each one. I realized that at the time I did what I thought was best. I decided that I couldn't turn back now. After tossing and turning all night I finally fell asleep. The next day I got up. It was difficult to do. It seemed that I was always ending up alone. I thought maybe this is where I'm suppose to be, alone....

CHAPTER 7

The Tragedy

"In September I started graduate school. I continued to work in the hospital. I moved from the receptionist area to the crisis unit. I only had class three times a week. I worked when I wasn't in school. I spent a lot of time studying.

On occasion I would accept an invitation from co-workers to go out. I enjoyed myself, but I wouldn't let myself get interested in any man that I met."

"Why is that?"

"I thought it best to concentrate on my career. That seemed to be the only sure thing.

In October my father called me. He asked if I could come home and help Carry. He said that she was having a hard time. She was suffering from Post Pardon Depression. Although I was hesitant about going I felt bad for Carry. I knew something about PPD. I wrote him back and said that I would come.

I decided to go during my winter break. I packed a

few things and got into my car. I headed back to that place I had no desire to ever return to. When I arrived at my father's home I knocked on the door. Yes I still had keys, but I didn't live there anymore. Carry opened the door. She hugged me. It felt like she was really happy to see me. While she hugged me Carry kissed me on the cheek and said that she had indeed missed me. I told her it was good to see her as well. She told me that my father was in the den. I asked where was the baby. I followed her upstairs. They had converted my old bedroom into a nursery, or should I say Carry did, because I knew my father never helped out around the house. When we entered the room the baby was awake. I asked if I could hold the baby. She said of course, he's your baby brother. I didn't respond. As I picked him up I thought how all of these innocent lives were younger than me. I was suppose to be this girls stepdaughter and I was older than she. I was suppose to be this baby's sister and I was so much older than he. Carry told me that she named him after my father. The baby stared into my eyes and smiled. I sat down and cradled him in my arms. Carry went to get a bottle. As I cradled the baby I prayed that God would watch over Terrance Jr. I asked God to keep him safe. I kissed Terrance and hugged him.

When Carry returned I asked her if she breast feed the baby. She said that she pumps her breast and put it into a bottle to feed the baby. She said that my father didn't approve of her breast feeding. He said that he didn't want her breast in anyone else's mouth. I just looked at her and took the bottle. I fed Terrance Jr. He was so beautiful. I told Carry that she did good. Carry looked tired, so I told her to go get rest and that I would take care of the baby.

I asked my father to put my twin mattress on the floor in the nursery, that I would be taking care of the baby while I was there."

"How did it feel to return home?"

"Home, it wasn't my home. It was a place where I grew up, because there was no other place to go."

"Did you ever think of telling anyone, of going to authorities?"

"I thought of it, but I was afraid that there may be a place worst. Crazy right? I thought that I might end up living on the street again. I was young, but I remembered me and my mother, how my mother was always on edge."

"Go on."

"The next day I took Terrance Jr. out for a walk. He seemed to enjoy it. As we were returning back to my father's home a car blew his horn. I looked. I didn't recognize the car so I kept walking. The car pulled up to the curb. The driver got out of the car. I was shocked to see Thomas' standing there. He walked over to me and hugged me. He kissed me on the cheek. The embrace was more than friendly. He seemed like he missed me. He released me and looked at the baby. He asked me if the baby was mine. I told him that he was my father's son. He seemed to be relieved. He then asked me how I was doing. I told him that I was fine and that I heard that he was in school. He smiled with pride and said that he had just graduated. I hugged him. The way he touched me when I hugged him made me long for him. He asked me what had I been up to. I told him that I had just graduated and that I was now in graduate school. He asked me what I was doing tonight. I told him nothing. He asked me if I would like to get a bite with him. I said sure.

When I returned to my father's home I informed Carry that I would be going out but I would take care of the baby until seven o'clock. Before getting ready to go out I fed Terrance Jr., bathed him and then put him to bed. I looked in on Carry. She was asleep. At seven I made sure the baby was asleep. I dressed quickly and by eight Thomas had pulled up to my father's house. I got into his car. Thomas looked so handsome. He looked even more handsome than I had remembered. His face had matured.

He drove to the restaurant. As we sat and ate we talked about what had been going on in our lives. Thomas was single and seemed to be happy that I was too. He asked me back to his place. I didn't hesitate to go. This was the first time that I had been in his apartment. He was living with his parents when I lived in Jersey. His apartment was neat and looked like a man's apartment. It was plain, nothing colorful, leather couch and love seat, a huge television and sport magazines under the coffee table. We sat in the living room. He offered me a drink. I accepted. We sat and drank wine. He asked me if I had moved back or was I moving back. I told him no, that I had only come up to help Carry. I told him about her condition. I told him that I would be returning to what I considered my home soon. I asked him if he ever thought of moving out of state. He stated that he hadn't. I asked him if he had dated since us. He answered no. I looked at him in disbelief. He told me that there had been a few women that he took out, but never anything serious. He asked me the same question. I told him about Charles.

He stared at me while I talked about my relationship with Charles. He asked me if I loved Charles. I told him that I found him interesting, that when I met him I was lonely. I told Thomas that I valued Charles intellect, but no I was not in love with him. I told Thomas that I couldn't get him out of my mine. Thomas gave me a questioning look. I asked him if he questioned my love for him when we were dating. He said that he questioned it when I wouldn't return. He went on to say that he believed that if I had truly loved him that I would have returned when he asked. He continued saying that now he understood that I had to do what I felt was most important for me. He confided that my determination was what made him go to school.

That night I dropped my guard, I wanted , no I needed someone to confide in. I decided that Thomas had always been more than someone I had made love to and more than a boyfriend. He was a friend. I started out by saying to him please don't think bad of me. I told him that my mother was fifteen when my father met her on the street. I told him that we were homeless and living on the street. I told Thomas that he was twenty at the time, had his own apartment and took us home. My real father didn't want anything to do with us. I told him that I had one picture of my mother. I confessed that she was beautiful. I told Thomas that I thought he was Prince Charming. I laughed, admitting that I thought I would live a fairy tale life. Thomas looked at me curiously. I told him that I know it's not funny, but it showed how naïve I was. Tears stream my eyes as I admitted that I truly thought that this man cared for my mother and that his caring for her would heal her, but it didn't. I informed Thomas that my mother only got sicker and my father moved her out of his room and into a guess room and that's when I became his wife. Thomas gave me a confused look. I continued. I was his wife, I cooked, cleaned and performed all wifely duties until I was ten years old. I told him that I became pregnant. He took me out of school until I had the baby. I had a baby girl. I lost her. She died at birth. I could see emotions in his eyes. I told him that I was happy that she wouldn't have to go through what I went through. I confided that I thought that he would do the same to her that he had to me. I told him that I was afraid that she would have taken my place and I couldn't bare to see my own child go through that. So yes I was ok with her death. I believed that God had spared us both.

I could see emotions in Thomas' posture. I continued telling him the reasons that I could not stay. I said to him that I thought something was wrong with me because all of these women truly loved my father and enjoyed having sex with him and actually felt pleasure. Thomas took my hands in his. He pulled me to him and held me. I began to cry. It felt strange because I had only cried once and that's when Cynthia left. Thomas held me tighter and kissed the side of my face. He told me that he was so sorry. I cried for an hour. When I got my composure I told him that I was sorry for breaking down. I further told him that I never cry. He looked at me and said that I had no reason to apologize.

It had gotten late. Thomas asked me if I wanted him to take me to my father's home. I said yes, because it would soon be time for Terrance Jr. to wake up to eat. Thomas looked at me. I told him that I knew Carry would still have to perform her wifely duties to my father and that she would be tired. I just wanted to take some pressure off her and I felt for the baby. He told me that he now understood my decision to move so far away and stay there.

He drove me back to my father's home. As I was getting out of the car he pulled me back. He kissed me with passion and something I had not felt before. I thanked him for listening. I went into my father's home. I grabbed a bottle for the baby and went up to Terrance Jr.'s nursery. He was awake. I picked him up and held him close and fed him. After he finished eating I patted him on the back to make sure that he didn't get gas. I rocked him until he fell asleep. Again I prayed over him before I layed him down. I layed on the mattress and thought about what I told Thomas. I wondered if his feelings would change from being my friend.

"How did you feel after that?"

"That night I felt such a relief. It was as if something had been lifted off my shoulders. I felt better that I had told someone and they hadn't thought less of me."

"Did he?"

"While I was visiting my father's home, when I wasn't taking care of the baby I spent my free time with Thomas. Things were different. We had both grown up and matured. We had a bond. Nothing that I had ever had, not even with Lori. I was not only in loved with this man, but I loved him deep within….."

"So did you decide to stay?"

"After two weeks past I packed my bags. I told Carry to call me if she ever needed me. When I left the house she actually seemed better. I drove to Thomas' apartment. I knocked on the door. He opened it. I told him this was it. I didn't care whether he felt the way I did or not. I had to tell him how I felt about him. I know that I had always lost guys after telling them, but I felt free. I told Thomas that I loved him and that I would always love him. I told him that no matter what happened I would always hold a special place in my heart for him and if he ever needed anything I would be there. He did not say anything. Thomas hugged me. In it I felt love. Although he did not confess it, I felt it in his touch.....

As I drove to what I called home I thought about my time with Thomas, I thought of Stephanie. I smiled thinking how she once told me that I would one day have that feeling of love for a man.

When I finally arrived to my new existence I studied harder than I ever had and when I wasn't studying I was working. I threw everything into what was now my new life. School took more work than when I was in undergraduate. I didn't go out much, partly because I was hoping that Thomas would want to be in my life so much that he would change his zip code and the other was to escape my loneliness.....

Several months went by. I received a letter from Carry. She thanked me for being there for her and that she always hoped that we would become friends. She then wrote that my father had begun acting different towards her. Fear and panic went through me. My hands trembled as I continued to read her letter. She said that she was taking her medicine for depression, but it wasn't working.

I wrote her back and told her to stay strong. I told her that if it would help that I would come to get the baby when I got out of school for the Summer.....

Some time went by without any word from Carry. I anxiously waited to hear from her. When a month had gone by and there was still no word I called her. I made sure that my father was not there. When Carry answered she sounded like she had been crying. I heard the baby crying in the background. I asked her what was wrong. She said that she hadn't seen my father for three days. He had stopped making love to her. I asked her what was wrong with the baby. She said that he was upset too. I asked her when he had last eaten. She couldn't tell me. I asked if she wanted to leave my father and come to live with me. She got quiet. I called her name and repeated my question. She said that she would stay there and work things out. She said that he needed someone to stay with him. She confided that everyone leaves him. I thought to myself, "Yeah and he wonders why." I didn't know what else to say to her other than feed the baby and that the offer still stands. It was quiet for a while. The silence went on for an hour. Then she said he's home. She said I'll call you later. I told her to take care.

On occasion Thomas would call me. My heart would leap when I heard his voice and sink when we would hang up....

Two months went by and I hadn't heard from Carry. I was concerned, but I figured that she would call if she needed to talk.....

By Spring I took a full time job and decided not to take any classes. I worked and saved money. My father still sent me money. In the envelope he would write that Carry said Hi. I was happy that Carry was doing alright.....

I called Thomas at the beginning of Summer. I invited him down, but he declined. I understood that he had his own life and that it didn't include me. I told myself that I would stop acting desperate. I started to do things by myself. I went to the beach by myself and visited museums. These things took me away from my lonely life. Sometimes I thought that maybe I should move back, but not stay at my father's home, but I needed to be in several states away from him.

In September I received a call from Carry. She told me that she was pregnant. I asked her how many months. She said that she was three months and was having a girl. I panic, but tried not to let it come through the phone. I tried to call her once a month. It seemed that things had changed. Each time that we spoke she was in a good mood.

One day she called and said that my father had gotten help with Terrance Jr. I asked her who was it. She told me that the girl was thirteen and had moved into the nursery with baby Terrance. I asked where did she come from. She told me that the girl was homeless. She said that the girl was nice and very helpful. I didn't want to say anything. I stayed in contact with Carry as much as I could......

When Carry was seven months she called me so excited. She told me that my father had eased up and let her rest. I couldn't believe that she didn't realize what was happening.

The next month she called and said that my father was so good to her, he wasn't bothering her about sex. He was letting her concentrate on her pregnancy. I still said nothing.....

In her ninth month my father moved down to the guest room. He wanted her to be comfortable. I didn't know how or if I should tell her what I suspected.

I tried to concentrate on my graduation. I was finishing

up and studying to continue to obtain my doctorates. I had two reports to do, so I worked on them.

A month past and I had not spoken with Carry. I still had not talked with her before she went to the hospital.

Carry called me when she got out of the hospital. She had the baby. Again she sounded happy. She said that my father had allowed her to breast feed. The baby stayed in the room with Carry. Carry said that my father was very nice to her and continued to let her bond with the baby.

She called me two months later and told me that the girl Tracy, who was staying with them had helped my father to convert the guest room into a nursery for their baby girl. She said that it was beautiful. Carry said that my father moved down to the den and moved Tracy in the guest room to let her get some more rest. She had started pumping her breast and Tracy took care of the babies. Tracy brought her food up to the room.

When the baby was five months Carry called to say all was well, but the baby girl was really red in her private part. I told her that I would leave school and come up. She told me not to worry, that they just needed to change the baby more. I didn't hear any more from Carry.

Although I worried about Carry and the babies I was busy with school.

Six months later I received a letter from Carry.

It read:

"Thank you for being my friend. I knew we would become friends. Too bad it wasn't before you moved. Monic I can't take it anymore Terrance hasn't touched me in over a year. I sometimes hear sounds at night, but I'm afraid to go see what it is. Sometimes I go

to check on the babies and Tracy is not upstairs. I sometimes hear her downstairs laughing with your father. The baby girl cries a lot and she is not getting better. Terrance won't let me take her to the doctor. He said that it's my fault that the baby cries, because I'm not being a good mother. I don't know what to do."

   Love Carry.

I wrote her back and told her to take the baby to the doctor. I told her that as soon as I get a break from school I would be up.

Two weeks later I received a letter from Carry saying:

   "Monic, I took the baby to the doctor. I told Tracy that I was taking her for a walk. The doctor said that he was going to run test and he would call me back. I think something's wrong."

Although I had my suspicions my heart sank when I read the letter.

I wrote her back and told her to be strong, that I would be up soon to get them.

The next letter read:

   "Monic I caught Terrance with Tracy twice, having sex. They didn't see me. I have started seeing her coming out of the den every morning. She's sleeping with him every night."

I did not return her letter. I began packing. I prayed

that things would not progress before I was able to get there.

I received another letter. It read:

"Monic I don't know what to do. Your father have put me out of our room and he and Tracy stay in there."

A fifth letter read:

"Monic the doctor called. He said that he was going to have to report that my daughter is being molested. What should I do?"

The last letter that I received said,

"Monic I stayed up last night. I heard your father and Tracy having sex and then Tracy went to get my daughter. She went back into your father's room. I think something awful is going on. Monic I don't know what to do.

Please help."

After that letter I got into my car. I only had the clothes that I was wearing. I went to the atm machine and got money. I drove all night. I was exhausted, but the adrenaline kept me going. I didn't know what I was going to do, but I had to do something. When I got to my father's home I knocked on the door. I didn't get any answer. I wondered if the police had come and taken everyone. Then I got a really sick feeling. I decided to use my key. I went into the kitchen.

There wasn't anyone there. I went into the den. That was empty as well. I went up to the babies' rooms. They were also empty. I shakily and slowly walked into my father's room. There laying on the bed was all of them. No one was breathing. I began to cry and I was having a hard time breathing myself. I called 911. I realized something was wrong with the air and decided to open windows. When the police came they told me to leave the house. After they had inspected the house they came out to talk to me. They asked me questions and then I asked them what happened. They said that they didn't know. They asked me where did I live. I told them. I gave them my address and phone number. I sat in my car watching as they took all of these souls out of my father's house. Tears flowed freely down my face. It was hours by the time the police left. When they had gone I went to lock my father's home up. Why I don't know. I began my long drive back to what was no longer feeling like home, but an empty escape.

Two weeks later I received a phone call from the cornier. He told me that my father and Tracy had been poisoned and the other members of the house died of carbon monoxide poisoning. I felt as if I was reliving that moment of finding them again. I thanked him, hung up the phone, then ran into my bathroom and threw up. I packed some bags. I don't know why, but I called Thomas. I told him what had happened and then asked him if I could stay a few days with him. He told me that I could stay as long as I needed.

I placed a bag in my car and headed by to New Jersey.

I returned to my father's house. I began clearing things out. I arraigned the funeral for all five of them. There wasn't anyone to invite, or that I wanted to know the horror of that house. I had the babies put in the casket with Carry. I couldn't advise her family because I didn't know who they were. I put my father in a plain casket. Nothing fancy. I purchased a beautiful dress that was age appropriate for Tracy and a beautiful casket to match her dress. She was a very lovely girl. I felt sorry for her tragic ending. I sat there alone thinking over my life and how all of the women who had been in my life, had tragically left it. I didn't know Tracy, but I've included her with those women. Throughout my life thus far I always thanked those women for saving me. Through saving me they lost their innocence and some their lives. I've grown to love these women, not so much because of spending time with, but because of the innocence that we all once shared and even though I don't and will never admit it again because we all loved my father.

After kissing Carry and her beautiful children, I went over to Tracy and smoothed my hand over her face. I wondered if there was anyone who would grieve for her. I kissed my fingers and then put them to her cheek. I walked over to my father and just stared at him. I wondered what kind of person could destroy so many lives. I still wonder if he ever loved any of us. I still wonder what or if anything had happened to him to have made him turn out the way he was.

After leaving the funeral home I returned to my father's home and began calling around to find a number for shelters for the homeless. I donated everything that was in the house to the homeless shelter. I put my father's house on the market. I went through my father's papers. He had left everything to me. I didn't realize that he had so much money. I donated his car to the children's home.

When I was done I called Thomas to make sure that he was home. When I arrived at his house I told him everything. He asked me why I had not called him so he could be there for me. I told him that I felt it was something that I had to do alone. I thanked him for caring and allowing me to stay at his place. He asked me where had I stayed. I told him that I slept in my car, outside of my father's home. I remained in town an additional week.

When I was ready to return Thomas asked me to stay. I told him that I had to sort things through. Before I left I informed the realtor to notify me when the place was sold. I also told her to sale it for whatever she could get.

CHAPTER 8

A New Beginning

I returned to my apartment. I returned to school. It was overwhelming. There was so much work for me to do and I was having a difficult time concentrating. My mind kept drifting back to my childhood. Then I would think of all of the young girls who had been abused in my father's home. I grieved for them and I grieved for my father. At the time I didn't understand why. I realized much later that I grieved for my father. The man who gave my mother and me shelter. The man who took care of my mother and her child, people who he didn't know. My father was kind to me. I did not grieve for my husband. When he died many years ago I was happy. I feared his ghost for a long time. Because of these feelings I asked my job for an extension. I had too much school work to do. I spent most of my time studying, trying to complete the mission that I had started so long ago.

Seven months later the realtor called me and said that she had found a buyer for my father's house. The house sold for half a million dollars. I donated a hundred thousand to a children's organization for exploited teens. The remainder was placed in a mutual fund. I still donate to this organization every year. I asked the realtor to look for an apartment for me. I decided to move back to Jersey. I figured since my father was gone, there was no reason to stay away.

After I received my doctorates I sold and donated all of my belongings that I had accumulated so I wouldn't have to take them with me. I wanted to begin a new. I packed my personal things up in one suit case. It was all I had left. I placed it in my trunk. I locked my apartment and drove to the rental agency. I turned in the key. I started on my way back to Jersey.

As I drove back I thought about my past. I felt bad that I had not gotten to Carry in time.

I never thought that she would do what she did. I wanted to help her, but I was too late. I thought about my father. He destroyed so many lives. I often wondered how he became the way he was. I used to pray that he would be heeled. I guess God let things take care of itself. Half way back to Jersey I decided to stop and sleep in a hotel. I didn't realize until it got late that I was so tired. I had not really rested since I visited my father's home, before the deaths. As soon as I got into my room I laid down and fell asleep.

I had a dream about my mother. She was dressed in white. She was so beautiful. I told her that I wished she was here with me. I told her that I was all alone now. I told her there were so many secrets that she never told me. My mother looked at me and said that they had never been told to her either. She told me that I was free now, that everything was going to be alright. She hugged me. I felt like a little girl in her arms.

When I woke up I felt good. I didn't feel the weight of the world on my shoulders anymore. I started out again. I tried to take in some of the scenery as I drove. As I got closer to New Jersey I felt panic, fear and some excitement. I was beginning a new life. I was all alone now. I had no family and only friends from high school that I hadn't maintained. Thomas and I had remained friends. Thinking about Thomas made my heart leap. I didn't want to get my hopes up, because I didn't know if he still wanted me the way he did so many years ago.

When I arrived in New Jersey I went over to the rental agency. I picked up my keys and went to my apartment. I walked in and looked around. The apartment was empty. I left the apartment and drove to a furniture store. I ordered furniture, but it wasn't going to be delivered until two days later. I purchased an air mattress. I went to another store and purchased linen. I was getting hungry, so I stopped at a Chinese restaurant and ordered take out.

I returned to my apartment and inflated my mattress. I put the covers on it and then ate. I put the leftovers in the refrigerator. I laid down and went to sleep.

The next day I got up and went shopping for clothes, shoes, house-wares, linen, curtains and food. I put up my food, curtains, clothes and everything else.

Monday the phone company came out, cable and my furniture. I arranged my furniture. I made a salad for dinner, read a little and then went to bed.

Tuesday I went art shopping. Charles had given me some pointers. I purchased several pieces, statues, vase and then went to purchase fresh flowers.

Wednesday I stayed in. By 4 p.m. I called Thomas. He asked me where was I calling from, because he noticed the number was local. I told him that I was at my apartment. He hesitated. I told him that I had just moved back. He asked me when did I get here. I told him five days ago. He asked me was I here to stay. I told him I was. I asked him if he was free on Friday. He said yes. I gave him my address and told him that I would cook. We talked for an hour and then got off the phone. Thomas said that he had to get up early the next morning.

Thursday I got up and went to the grocery store. I purchased food to cook for Friday. Then I went to the liquor store and purchased champagne. I wanted to celebrate because I felt free. I purchased a news paper. I decided to go clothes shopping to get some clothes for lounging, lingerie and an outfit for Friday. I wanted to get something sexy, but didn't want to look like I was trying.

When I got home I put the food up and then put the clothes up. It was getting late so I decided to go to bed. Friday morning I got up and straightened up my apartment. I took the food out that I was going to prepare. I fixed me a light breakfast and sat down and ate.

After eating I cleaned the kitchen and then went to prepare the clothes that I was going to put on later.

At two o'clock I started cooking. Thomas was coming over at 5:30. When the food was in the oven, I put on some music, set the dinning room table and placed the champagne to chill on the table. I went to check on the food again and then went to get dressed. I took my time to smooth lotion all over my body. I sprayed perfume onto my undergarments, put on my stockings and attached them to my garter. I put on my dress. It was a basic black dress that was form fitting. Nothing flashy, but it was feminine. I put a chocker on to match the dress. The chocker had a pearl surrounded by small rhymes stones. I put on earrings to match. I took the food out and placed it in bowls. I placed them on the table. The door bell rang. I ran and put on my strap up shoes and then went to the door. I opened the door. The way Thomas looked at me made me blush. I couldn't help smiling. I reached out and hugged him. He said that I looked good. He kissed me lightly. It was nice. I told him to follow me and that dinner was ready. I told him to have a seat and I opened the champagne.

He asked me what was all of this. I told him that I was celebrating my new life. I explained over dinner that for so many years I was always afraid. I held onto secrets, shame and regret. That was over now. I told him that I was beginning a new life and I was going to enjoy it. I wanted to tell him that I wanted it to be with him, but I held back. I didn't want him to feel uncomfortable or forced into anything that he wasn't ready for or wanted. He held his glass up and said, well lets toast to your new life, may you find all the happiness that you deserve and all the passion that you desire. He winked at me. We toast and then sipped the champagne. We ate dinner and then I brought out the dessert. Thomas jokingly said, what are you trying to do to me. You come to the door dressed like that, serve me a delicious dinner, serve champagne and make a desert which taste provocative. I told him that I just wanted him to share in my happiness. He said that he felt privileged to be the one I chose to share my celebration with.

After dessert I told him to come into the living room. We sat and talked about the future. I told him that next week I would start to look for a job. He told me about his job. Out of the blue he asked me have I ever thought about getting married and having children. I told him that I have and hoped to one day be blessed with a loving, mentally healthy man, get married and have healthy children. I asked him the same thing. He said that he thought he had found his wife once, but she wasn't ready. I wanted to ask him who she was, what happened and was it me, but I was afraid of what his answer would be.

CHAPTER 9

The Beginning of
a New Romance

After our dinner Thomas asked me if I wanted to try us again. I could have jumped up and down, but I played it cool and said casually that I would. We sipped on the champagne and talked all night. He left at one in the morning. It felt so nice, just talking. We never touched, but I felt sparks throughout the night.

We spent the rest of the weekend going to the movies on Saturday, eating out and going to church on Sunday. Even though it was never spoken, we wanted to take the relationship slow. The only kiss that we did was a light one when we greeted each other. I think we both knew that if we actually touched anymore than that we did and kissed we would be lost.

The next week we only talked on the phone a few times. I was busy searching for a job and he was working. I looked forward to the weekend. We had a date. We planned to go dancing on Friday.

When Friday came I prepared my clothes for the night. I rested a bit so I would be fresh when Thomas came to pick me up.

At 6 o'clock I began getting dressed. I put my hair up. I dressed sexy, but comfortable. I remembered Thomas liked to dance. I didn't want my hair getting too wet.

At 8 o'clock Thomas came to pick me up. We went to get something light to eat and then went to the club. When we entered the club we found a seat in a corner of the club where there wasn't too many people. We ordered drinks. When we finished our drinks Thomas asked me if I wanted to dance. I stood up and we went out onto the dance floor. I could tell Thomas had not stayed home while we were apart. He was up on the new dances. We danced to a few songs.

After a while we decided to sit back down. We laughed and talked. It was really nice sitting with this attractive man. Although Thomas and I had dated in the past this was different. He had matured. He had become a confident man. The way he walked and talked showed this.

After having a few drinks Thomas and I danced a few more times before the club closed. As Thomas drove me home we were quiet. I looked out into the night sky thinking how different things looked. I felt unbelievably good.

When we arrived in front of my house Thomas parked. I lightly kissed him goodnight. I didn't want him to leave, but we knew that he had to. I went into my apartment.

Once in my apartment I began taking off my clothes. I went into the bathroom and got into the shower. As I washed my body I thought of Thomas. I thought of how good it would feel to have him share my shower. I turned off the shower and dried off. Just as I was about to lay down the telephone rang. I picked it up. My heart leaped. He told me that he just wanted to hear my voice once more before he fell asleep. He said good night and we hung up. That night I slept better than I ever had.

We took up to going out dancing every Friday. I came to look forward to Fridays. This is when Thomas held me close on the slow songs and teasingly danced up on me during the fast ones. Sometimes Thomas would attend church with me. On those occasions the minister would make a point in coming over to talk to us. I believe that he saw something promising. I at least hoped it.

A year had gone by Thomas and I had no more than lightly kissed hi and goodbye. I longed for his touch, but waited patiently for Thomas to make a move. There were times that I thought I saw something and that he would make a move but he didn't.

One Friday Thomas came over as usual and picked me up. He greeted me the usual way. We left my apartment and headed out to eat. The waiter came to greet us. When the waiter looked at me he asked if I remembered him. I didn't, but after a few minutes of him probing I recalled graduating with him. He said it was good to see me and took our order.

After he left Thomas commented on the way the waiter looked at him. I dismissed it. Thomas for the first time told me that I was his. I looked at Thomas surprised. Although we had expressed that we were dating a year ago Thomas had not made any attempts to be intimate or said anything to show any emotions.

After we ate our meal Thomas and I left the restaurant.

On the way out the door the waiter said that it was nice to see me again. I thought it was amusing when Thomas placed his arm around my waist. I enjoyed this and wished that he did it more often. Thomas opened the car door and I got in. We were quiet during our drive to the club.

After an half hour of quiet we arrived at the club. Thomas parked the car and we got out. Thomas took my hand and we walked to the front of the club. Holding his hand felt nice. His hands were so strong. They were large and made me feel good about being a woman. He opened the door to the club and I walked in. We immediately went onto the dance floor. As we danced Thomas held my waist. I saw something different in Thomas that night. He was more attentive. I liked it. I teasingly danced up on him and then away. We sat resting some of the night and had drinks. Thomas stayed close. This he had not done since I had returned to Jersey.

When the club closed Thomas drove me home. When we pulled up in front of my apartment Thomas parked. We sat a few minutes remaining quiet. Things had changed between us. It was strange. It seemed like we were on our very first date. I finally broke the silence and said, "I had a great time." I reached over and kissed him lightly on the lips. Thomas placed his hand behind my neck, held my head to his face. He leaned in and kissed me. His strength mesmerized me. Although he only held the back of my neck it was like fireworks. He stopped abrupt and said good night.

I got out of the car and went into my apartment. When I got in my apartment the phone rang. I picked it up. It was Thomas. He asked if I was ready for the night to end. My heart leaped, I smiled to myself and said no.

He asked if he could come in. I told him yes. I went to the door and opened it. Thomas came in. I went into the kitchen and got us something to drink. We sat and talked. Thomas got up and moved to the love seat where I was sitting. He cupped my face, he moved closer and kissed me. He then put one of his arms around my waist and pulled me even closer. I placed my arms around his neck. As we kissed he caressed my back. His touch felt so good. We kissed a while. Thomas sat back and positioned me across him. He told me that he couldn't take it any more. He had to touch me. I layed in his arms. He kissed me again, holding me close to his chest. I held onto him and caressed the back of his neck. Thomas smoothed his hand down my body sending sparks throughout it. He kissed my neck and then whispered I got to have you. He picked me up and carried me over to the coach. He layed me down and then layed beside me. He caressed and teased my body. It felt so good that I wanted it to last forever. I pulled him to me and we kissed. I began to unbutton his shirt. He allowed me to remove it. I then unbuttoned his pants and unzipped them. He stood up to remove his pants and then stopped. He asked me if I was sure. I answered by pulling my blouse over my head. He removed his pants. He unbuttoned my pants and pulled them off. He admired my lingerie. He laid next to me and caressed my body. He nibbled on my lips and ran his tongue across them. I basked in this moment not wanting this feeling to end. Thomas continued to kiss and caress me. I moaned as he cupped my breast and nibbled on them. I then took control and began to caress and tease his body. He caressed my hair as I moved down his body. Thomas pulled me up to him. I layed on top of him. As he slowly moved his body he looked into my eyes. He smiled as he saw passion in them. He watched as I longed for this feeling. I too looked into his eyes and watched his expression as he struggled to stay in control. He continued to move erotically under me. I matched his movements. We kissed and caressed until finally Thomas completed me. It was such pleasure to be one with him. We started slow wanting to capture every delicious feeling. It was if our bodies had missed each other. Thomas whispered to me as he moved slowly. It was as if he was trying to stay controlled. On occasion he would tell me how he felt. I took delight in this. I had never been told how I made him feel. As the sun came up our bodies completed our journey. We collapsed and drifted off to sleep in each others arms.

I awakened to Thomas kisses. He was still aroused. He turned me over on my back and began to caress my body. As he touched me my body responded. Thomas caressed me until I called out his name. He answered my call and we were one, lost in the pleasures of our bodies. My body rose and fell as Thomas and I moved together. I held onto him, my mind reeling from so much pleasure. Thomas' body soon lost control and he melted into me. He laid there a while, me holding onto him not wanting our bodies to be apart. We fell back to sleep.

When we woke up again it was three in the afternoon. The day had continued as we slept. I kissed Thomas and he eased off of me. We ordered food and Thomas went to pick it up.

When he returned he had the food and a dozen of roses, eleven white and one red. He handed them to me and kissed me. We sat in the den, made a picnic on the floor, I placed the roses near me and we ate. Throughout the meal I looked at them. I had never received roses before. Thomas didn't realize how special those roses were. When we were done Thomas took my hand. He said, "Monic I am in love with you. I have been for a long time. I should have done this a long time ago, but I didn't and I almost lost you. You've been my lover and friend, now will you do me the pleasure of becoming my wife."

I looked at him in disbelief. I looked into his eyes to see if he was joking. His eyes were true. I sat up on the chair. I was in shock. I never expected him to ask me, not now anyway. My mind flashed back to my first husband and for a minute I moved back out of panic. He continued to sit on the floor waiting for my answer. I regained control and scolded myself for acting like a victim. I sat back on the floor and took his hands. I saw the worried look on his face. I smiled reassuringly and said yes. He continued to sit there. I guess out of shock or maybe to process my answer. He asked was I sure and again I said yes. He pulled me to him and kissed me. We sat there for a while just holding onto each other.

When we both recovered from the shock we began to discuss our future. We decided to have a small wedding. We made plans for me to meet his parents. We didn't want to wait very long so we made a date to get married in six months.

It was two weeks since Thomas had asked me to marry him. We were to go to dinner at his parents' place. I was so nervous. Thomas came over to pick me up. He saw that I was nervous and told me to calm down.

As we drove to his parent's home I thought about my life, my past. I thought it's amazing how when you're happy your regrets come creeping back up trying to steal your joy. As we got closer to their home Thomas must have sensed my fear. He took my hand in his and told me that everything was going to be fine. He told me that no one had to know about my past. He said when they ask about your parents just tell them that they passed away. He said we don't have to tell them anything else unless you want to. He let go of my hand and cupped my face. He turned my face towards his. He looked away from the traffic a brief second to tell me that he wasn't ashamed of my past, that he saw me as courageous. He laughed and said you're my hero and I love you unconditionally. He pulled my face to his and kissed me. I layed my head on his chest. His words made me feel better, but I was still nervous.

I thought what if his family didn't like me, would he change his mind about us getting married. Once again I felt alone. I had no one to come to the wedding. I would be trapped with his family and if they didn't approve of me I would be miserable.

When we pulled into their driveway Thomas got out of the car. He walked over to my side and opened the door. He held his hand out to me and I took it. He put one arm around my waist and the other held my hand and we walked to the front door. When the door opened his mother hugged Thomas and then me. She took me by the hand and said it's nice finally meeting you. She said come on in, have a seat, dinner will be ready in just a minute. She asked me if I would like something to drink. I told her juice if she had any. She gave me a look. Thomas noticed the look and said no mother. Soon after she brought me the juice she announced that dinner was ready. Just as we were about to sit down to eat the doorbell rang. It was Thomas' twin sisters. One seemed ok, the other I couldn't get a read on.

We ate dinner and discussed the wedding. I asked Thomas' sisters if they wouldn't mine being in my wedding. They both seemed genuine in their delight. They perked up after that. They gave me their phone numbers and I gave them mine. The rest of the night went smoothly. Thomas' mother seemed to warm up to me when I asked for her help. As it got late Thomas announced that we had to leave. Although I was enjoying myself I was ready to leave. His family and I hugged and said our goodbyes. As we drove back to my apartment Thomas and I made plans to talk with our minister.

The next week was busy. Between looking for employment, meeting Thomas' mother and picking out the invitations and getting them out I was exhausted. Thomas and I spent Saturday in. We ordered take-out and watched movies. He stayed over and we went to church. After the service we met with the minister. We discussed available dates and times. He sent us to the couple's counselor to arrange dates for a week section. When this was done we drove to my apartment and surf the internet for halls. We called several halls and made appointments to visit them. Thomas left at midnight.

The next morning I got up, dressed and went out to look for my wedding dress. As I was walking through the mall I ran into Cynthia. We hugged. She asked me how I was doing. I asked her how she was. She said that she was great. She had a daughter and was living with the father. She asked me about my father. I told her what happened. Her eyes got watery. She told me that she was sorry for my lost. I didn't feel any lost. I couldn't believe that Cynthia really did love my father. I told her thank you. We hugged and then parted. As I walked away I hoped that she found a good man and that she was happy. I continued looking for my dress. Two hours later I entered a small boutique. They didn't have many dresses, but they had a book of gowns. As I searched through the book I finally saw what I was looking for. I ordered the gown. I was told that it would take seven working days.

While I waited for the shop to call me about my dress Thomas' sisters, Sherry and Kristina went to look for Bridesmaid dresses. We finally found a dress that we all liked. We went to dinner afterwards. They talked about Thomas and told me things about his childhood. They were surprised that Thomas and I had known and dated for so long. When the dinner was over we scheduled to meet again for their fitting and have lunch.

A week had past. Monday morning the shop called me to tell me that my dress had arrived. I finished eating and then dressed. I then left for the boutique. When I got there the store owner was waiting excitedly. She said that she was afraid that the dress would not look like the picture, because it had happened before and she had to send it back. The lady took the cover off the dress. I couldn't believe it. The dress was more beautiful than anything I'd ever seen. I walked up to the dress, just looking at it, almost afraid to touch it. It was white, made with pearls and rime stones and with beautiful lace. I shakily touched it. The store owner told me to remove my clothes. I did as I was told. I felt guilty putting the dress on because I felt that I wasn't clean enough to put it on. I thought of my past. I wasn't a virgin by no way. I stepped into the dress. It fitted perfectly. I smoothed my hand over the dress. The store owner marveled at it's perfection. She said that I made her job easy. She said that all she had to do is put a hem in it. As I looked in the mirror I was amazed at how good it fitted. I smiled thinking about how I was going to be marrying Thomas soon. I was happy that the gown only needed slightly hemming and it would be ready in two days. The shop owner helped me take the dress off. I was very careful. I didn't want to do anything to mess the dress up.

When I got home I checked my messages. There was one. I played it. I was asked to come to an interview. I was so excited. I had been looking for a job for sometime now. I called the person back and was scheduled to come in on Wednesday. I immediately went into my closet and looked to find something to wear. I pulled out a blue dress suit and took it to the cleaners. Tuesday I went back and picked it up. I went home and cooked a light dinner for two. Thomas was coming over. When he got to my place I told him about the interview. He was happy for me and reassured me that I would get it. He wanted to leave early so I would get some rest, but I convinced him to stay over. I was nervous and I knew waking up in his arms would help me to know my life was coming together. Thomas awakened early and got dressed. He had began leaving clothes for occasions such as this. He wrote me a note and left for work. When I awakened the note was on the pillow next to me. It said, "Good luck, have confidence that you are the best for the company. Call me when your interview is over. Love you." I kissed the note, had a little breakfast and began getting dressed.

Once I was dressed I left and headed to my interview.

I was so nervous. I prayed all the way there and when I arrived at the building I took a moment and meditated. I continued to pray as I walked to the building. When I entered I got on the elevator and pressed the button for the eleventh floor. I walked into the office and continued to the receptionist area. I was told to have a seat. I waited about fifteen minutes and then was greeted by the woman who had called me for the interview. She escorted me into the office. The interview was nothing like I expected. We talked about how to treat different types of mental illness. It was as if we were colleagues. After an hour I was asked if I had time to speak with her partner. Of course I said I did. After a half hour Colleen's business partner came out to meet me. The three of us discussed their business plan. We talked for an hour.

After the hour I was asked to stick around a little while longer. Fifteen minutes went by and the receptionist escorted me back to Colleen's office. When I got in Jim, Colleen's partner stood up and held his hand out. He said we would like to offer you a position. I couldn't believe it. I accepted the position. Colleen escorted me to the office manager, Evelyn. Evelyn took my information and made copies of my id. When I left I walked quickly to my car. It was four o'clock, I wanted to get to Thomas before he got off of work. His phone rang twice. He answered. I yelled I got it. He said I told you. He told me to get dressed that we were celebrating tonight. When I got home I took several outfits out and then I spotted the perfect one. Thomas arrived at seven. He looked so good in his grey suit. He came over and hugged me. We left for the restaurant. When we arrived at the restaurant Thomas ordered wine. When the waiter returned with our wine we ordered dinner. While we waited for our dinner I told Thomas about the interview and about the job. When the food came we ate and I continued to tell him about the interview. I then told him that I met with his sisters and picked out their dresses. He asked me what I had planned for Friday. I told him nothing. He told me to keep it that way. After dinner we returned to my place. We undressed and just laid in each other's arms. The next morning Thomas kissed me and got out of bed. He dressed, kissed me lightly and left for work. I fell back to sleep.

When I awakened I cleaned up my apartment, went through my clothes closet and decided that I needed to get clothes for work. I dressed and went out shopping. I purchased ten suits, blouses, lingerie stocking and shoes. I stopped at the grocery store and bought food to stock my cabinets When I got home, I put my clothes up and then cooked dinner. Just as I was fixing my plate and putting it down, I went towards the front of the house, Thomas had made his way halfway to the kitchen. I jumped when I saw him. He asked me why did I jump. I told him that I didn't know that he was coming over. He told me that he wanted to surprise me. I told him that I was just getting ready to eat and offered him dinner. He told me to sit. He fixed himself a plate and sat down next to me. We ate. He told me that he had taken Friday off because he wanted to take me somewhere. I was curious. I asked him where were we going, but he insisted on surprising me. We sat and talked about where we were going to live. We talked throughout the night. We went to bed and layed in each others arms. He caressed my hair and shoulders. I thought how wonderful his touch was and how I wanted to wake up every day to this touch. I drifted off to sleep with my head nestled in his chest. The next morning we woke up. Thomas kissed me and I returned the passion.

When we finally got up I fixed us a light breakfast and then we headed to my surprise. We drove for thirty minutes and then stopped in front of a shopping center. Thomas parked and turned off the car, walked over to my side of the car and helped me out of the car. After getting out of the car Thomas lead me to a jewelry store. He talked to the jeweler and a few minutes later the jeweler brought out a ring box and showed it to me. He told me it was specially made, that Thomas had come up with the design. Then he gave the box to Thomas. Thomas opened it. I looked inside the box. It was his and her matching wedding bands. In a second box was a beautiful two carat remarkable designed engagement ring. Neither of the rings were anything I could have ever imagined. I hugged Thomas. Thomas returned my embrace and said I guess you like my surprise. I said like it. I love it. He placed it on my finger. He put the other box in his pocket. Thomas and I left the store and we decided to go to a mortgage company. We got approved for a mortgage. Thomas knew a realtor, so when we left the mortgage company and got in the car he called him. He made an appointment for us to come in Saturday. When he got off the phone we went to lunch. I smiled all through lunch. I couldn't believe how happy I was. We ate lunch and discussed the type of home, size, land and number of bedrooms. We talked about having children. After lunch we drove around for a while looking at different areas, discussing which neighborhoods we would consider.

When we arrived back at my place we were exhausted. We laid on the bed. Thomas laid on his back and I placed my head on his chest. We soon drifted off to sleep. It was 8 o'clock when we woke up. Thomas ordered Chinese food. We made a picnic on the floor and ate dinner. We watched a movie afterwards and then went to bed. The next morning we got up, went out to eat and then headed to the real estate office. Thomas told me that we were meeting a Dennis Miller. When we got there the receptionist told us to have a seat, that Dennis had just stepped out to his car. After fifteen minutes of waiting Dennis came in the door. My back was turned. Thomas stood up and shook his hand. Thomas motioned to me and said this is my fiancé. As I turned I couldn't believe my eyes. It was my Dennis. The first boy that I had made love to. The first boy I told that I loved. When I stood up, he recognized me and he smiled broadly. He took my hand and held it as he said nice to meet you. Thomas had told me that they knew each other from their old neighborhood. As Thomas and I described what we were looking for Dennis on occasion would give me a lingering look. He managed to ask if we were living together. Thomas didn't see anything unusual in the question. He told him that we each had our own apartment. Dennis then asked if we had any children and explained that would help in showing us the best house. Thomas answered that we didn't have any but planned to. He lovingly touched my hand which was relaxing on my leg. Dennis probed further. He asked for our addresses and for my phone number in case he couldn't reach Thomas. Again Thomas thought nothing of it and I questioned it myself, thinking maybe I was reading more into it then I should. Dennis turned his attention to his computer, wrote down a few addresses and then told us that he would like to show us a couple of places. We were excited. We all got up. We got into Dennis Mercedes. As we drove Dennis asked how long we had dated and did we have a wedding date. On occasion Dennis looked through his rear view mirror at me. It wasn't a casual look. It was a more questioning look. I tried to look out the car window.

When we arrived at the first house Dennis opened the door and motioned for us to enter. We looked around, at first together and then Dennis took Thomas down to the finished basement, to show him the pool table. While they were down there I went up to the second level where the bedrooms were. While I was in the master bedroom Dennis came up. He said how good I looked and that I had really grown into a beautiful woman. I thanked him. He began showing me the features in the bedroom. Soon after Thomas came up. Dennis showed Thomas the features in the room. We continued the tour throughout the house. We really liked the house, but we wanted to look at the other two before we made our decision.

The next house was larger. We walked through the house and it also had a finished basement, but nothing had been placed in it. As Dennis discussed the possibilities with Thomas I went back up stairs. I went into the kitchen. I loved the kitchen. Soon Thomas and Dennis came upstairs and came into the kitchen. Dennis asked if I liked to cook. Thomas said "Man my fiancé can throw down." He hugged me from behind. Dennis looked away to shield his expression, but I caught it as he said really. He looked envious. We left this place and also considered it.

The third place was even larger. The ceilings were high and I always loved high post beds. I imagined the furnishing that I would purchase for the house. The kitchen was very similar to the second place, but on a grander scale. It had granite counter tops, a huge island with a sink made in it. It had two ovens, a build in microwave and the cabinetry was beautiful. They were cherry wood, with some of the cabinets made with glass. Nothing I had ever seen. There was a eating area off of the kitchen that lead to glass sliding doors and a patio that I had only seen in magazines. As we went through the house Thomas was aware of how much I liked it. When we were leaving Thomas said take this off the list. Dennis said to me so this is it. I said yes. He gave me another look. I wasn't sure what it meant. We left and went back to the agency. Dennis casually shook Thomas hand and then took my hand in both his and said it was a pleasure, still holding my hand, he then said he looked forward in doing business we us and that we could call him any time, and he put emphasis on night or day. Thomas told him that we were going to discuss the three houses and get back to him. We left and headed back to my place. We discussed the house.

When we got to my apartment I cooked dinner for us. As we ate Thomas said that he was impressed how quick Dennis had warmed up to me and how friendly he was. I wondered if I should tell him that I once had a relationship with Dennis. After Thomas went on about Dennis behavior I told him, I said I guess I didn't feel comfortable telling him about past relationships, especially those that included me having sex with them. He took it well. He said that he didn't expect me to not have a past, but if we ever run into someone else that I already knew he would appreciate me telling him. He then asked me if I was comfortable with keeping him as a realtor. I told him that I didn't have a problem with him. I further told him that it wasn't really a past. Thomas said ok. We then made a decision to purchase the third house. Thomas called Dennis and told him. Dennis called the seller's realtor.

The next week Dennis called my cell phone. It was six o'clock. Thomas wasn't due to come by. He was working late. Dennis asked if Thomas was with me. I told him no. I asked if he had called Thomas. Dennis said that he had been trying to reach him for a couple of hours. I told him that Thomas was working late and asked him if there was anything that I could do. Dennis said as a matter of fact I could. He said that he was out side of my apartment and asked if he could come in. I said sure. I looked out the window and sure enough Dennis was out there. I opened the door. He came in. He said that everything was going well, he just wanted to drop some paper work by and he thought that Thomas would be here. I told him that it was alright. He handed me the paper work and then took my hand. He said can I talk to you for a minute. I asked him what about. Still holding my hand he said I would first like to apologize. I asked him for what. He said about how he left our relationship. I told him not to worry about it. He said really I didn't know what to do when you told me that you were falling in love with me. I said really don't think about it. That it was a long time ago and I got over it.

He moved in closer and said, "You are so beautiful. I can't believe that I let you slip through my fingers. Monic is there any way that we can start where we left off."

I said that we have. He looked at me puzzled and then moved in closer. I put my hand on his chest and said, We are standing here, you working for me and my fiancé. Our

relationship ended many years ago. I have to thank you for going your way, because I met a wonderful man. It has been flattering for you to still be attracted to me, after all of these years that's as far as it goes. I love Thomas and I will not have anything come between us. I told him about us. Now you need to leave, because nothing is going to happen between us, but business."

Just as I went to turn around to walk Dennis out, Thomas was standing there. He looked angry. I had never seen him angry before. He walked up to Dennis. Thomas asked Dennis, "Man what's going on?"

Dennis said, "Man I brought some paper work by."

Thomas asked, "Man why are you lying?

Dennis said "Ask Monic."

I gave him the papers. Thomas got in Dennis' face and said, "I heard everything you said to Monic. I thought we were friends. Why would you try this?"

Dennis said, "Man I had her first. Our thing never ended.

Thomas said with base in his voice and point blank, "That's it. You only had a thing. Further more you didn't recognize what you had. I have. We're getting married and if you ever disrespect me or my fiancé again we are going to have a problem." Thomas then looked at me and said, "Do you want to fire him?" I looked at Dennis and said no. Thomas then turned his attention back to Dennis and said, "You are only to contact me. If you can't reach me leave a message. You are not to contact Monic unless I authorize you to do so." He then said do you understand. Dennis shook his head in agreement and then apologized. Thomas and Dennis shook hands. Denni looked at Thomas and said do you mind? Thomas nodde

Dennis took my hands in his and said I do apologize for everything. He also said I wish you every happiness. I told him thank you. As he and Thomas walked to the door I thought of Dennis' expression when he wished me well. He looked like he truly meant it. Thomas stayed outside with Dennis for a while. I was curious as to what they were talking about, but I didn't want to appear interested. When Thomas came in he kissed me on the lips and then asked me if I was alright. I told him that I was fine. I casually stated that he and Dennis was outside a long time. Thomas told me that he had to let Dennis know that he was wrong and there was some other things that he couldn't share with me. I felt proud and comforted that there was someone that I could rely on. I kissed him and told him as much.

CHAPTER 10

On The Job

My first day at work was interesting. I met all of the staff. I was shown around and given my office. My office is huge and I love the privacy. I was given records of several clients that I would be working with. I wasn't able to look through the files until after lunch, because of orientation. At three o'clock my boss Angelica came in and told me that she would go over each case the next day. The clients weren't due to come in until the next month. I was happy about this because I had very little experience counseling. I had interned, but there was always someone guiding me and I didn't really seem responsible for the client's treatment. After I got off of work I returned home. I took a warm shower and was too exhausted to eat anything.

The next morning I awakened earlier. I decided to discuss the time that I would need off in three months. When I got to work I went into my office and because I was the first there I went through some of the papers that were given to me during orientation. I wanted to get familiar with my surroundings. It felt good. As the staff came to work they stopped in my office and spoke to me. When Angelica came in she stopped in my office. She asked if we could talk. Angelica took the client's records and began looking through and going over the treatment plan. It was lunch time when she pulled her head up and asked me for my input. I took this time to talk about the time off that I needed. She didn't have a problem with the time. She seemed excited and wished me well with my wedding. At four Angelica knocked on my door. I told her to come in. She peeped her head in and asked me was I ready. I got up and we caught the elevator together. She asked me how was I getting along. I told her everything was fine.

On the way home I picked up a couple of meals. I didn't feel like cooking. Thomas was do to come over. I came in and changed clothes. I hung up my suit and then went through the mail. Thomas came in the door. He greeted me with a kiss and asked me about my day. I told him that all the people seemed friendly. I also told him that I informed them of our wedding. He took me by my waist and pulled me close and said yeah. He kissed me. I told him not to start anything. We sat down and ate.

After eating we dressed and went to couples pre marriage class. I found it to be interesting. We did some exercises. At first I was kind of resistant, but they proved to be fun. After we left we returned to my apartment. Thomas had begun to stay at my place more. I enjoyed it. I liked waking up with him. We took a shower together and then went to bed. For the next two months that was our routine. Work was fine. I got along with all of the staff. I had five clients. Colleen and I sometimes went out to lunch. I ended up inviting her and all of the staff to the wedding. I didn't have anyone on my side anyway. The next month was hectic. We closed on the house a month before we moved in. We wanted to wait until we were married to move in. We ordered furniture, pictures, and decorated. We were careful not to order too many dishes because of our wedding. We had finished our couple session and I volunteered to help out with the session when we return from our honeymoon. I thought that I could be of assistance. I needed to help others.

Three weeks before I was to leave for my wedding and honeymoon I got a new client. When the lady came in she looked familiar, but I couldn't place the face. As we talked I kept trying to think of how I knew her. When the lady mentioned her daughter it came to me. Her daughter name was Tracy. The woman was very distraught. She said that she sold her daughter to a man once a week for crack. Tracy was twelve at the time. She said that when Tracy was thirteen they were homeless and she finally let her daughter go to live with him for $10,000.00. She said that she was really strung out. She thought she had hit the jack pot. After smoking up all of the money she ended up in the hospital. The woman chuckled to herself and then said it wasn't funny. She said that she was laughing because she ended up in the hospital before she got to use all of the drug. She had gotten hold of some bad stuff. The woman said that several months had gone by when she finally began thinking of where she was. In one of her meetings she realized what she had done. The woman said that she went back to the place where the horrible act was done, where she sold her baby. She talked to some of the people who she knew when she was out there. One woman remembered and gave her a clue. She tracked down where her daughter was staying, but by the time she found it, it was too late, Tracy was dead. I handed the woman some Kleenex and told her I was sorry. The woman thanked me for my kind words, but little did she know that I was apologizing and sorry for my father. I sat there listening to her story of how she had been abused when she was a child. I remained silent because I knew that this woman needed to get everything out in the air. I didn't think that she needed any words of wisdom. I didn't know if I had any. This woman came once a week for two weeks. I had her scheduled to come back in one month. My last day at work the office gave me a bridle shower. I was surprised. They gave me various gifts, from house wares to lingerie. I was shocked that some of the lingerie was really out there. It was nice that they took the time to do this for me. I left work a couple of hours early and headed home.

CHAPTER 11

The Wedding

When I arrived home. I went into my bedroom. I spotted a 'Thomas' shirt on my chase. I walked over to it and picked it up. I held it close. I could still smell his cologne. I loved the way Thomas smelled. I hugged his shirt and then laid it back on the chair where I found it. Thomas and I agreed not to see each other for a week before the wedding. I missed him, but I thought it was a good idea. I tried to keep myself busy and spent that time getting my clothes ready for the wedding and honeymoon. Thomas and I talked on the phone every other night. I looked forward to those moments, but it made me long for him more. He must have heard it in my voice because every time we were getting off the phone he would say soon.

The night before the wedding my soon to be sister-in-laws and mother-in-law came over to stay with me. They threw me a "Bachelorette" party. Sherry and Kristina invited their friends over. We played games. I was surprised that they knew many things about my likes and dislikes. I was moved that they took the time to get to know some things about me. As the evening drew to an end the door bell rang. Sherry went to answer it. As she opened the door Kristina turned music on and this six foot guy, very muscular and "Chocolicious" came in the door and began dancing. He asked who the bride was and everyone pointed to me. I stood frozen, shocked. He came close to me and bent down. He danced on his knees making sexual gestures. Embarrassed I covered my face. The dancer sensed my discomfort and moved back. He played to the others coming back to me on occasion. At one point Thomas' mother left the room. When the exotic dancer had finished he thanked me for being a good sport. The guest went home. Thomas' family and I stayed up until 3 a.m. Sherry and Kristina slept on my couch. Thomas' mother and I shared my bed. I must have been tired because it didn't take long for me to fall asleep.

The next morning I woke up kind of tired, but when I thought of what the day was gave me new found energy. I got out of bed, took a shower, fixed breakfast for my guest and myself. My guest awakened when they smelt the food. They got up and came into the kitchen. I fixed our plates. We talked as we ate. I thanked them again for their kindness. Thomas' mother told me that's what family do and that I am part of their family now. I smiled. I thought to myself how I have never had any family. I was happy that Thomas' family seemed to like me and were nice people.

After we ate they helped me clean the kitchen. When we were done we began to get dressed. I couldn't believe that I was getting married and to Thomas. At one time I thought I had lost him. I thought that this day will be the beginning of my happiness. Thomas' mother was dressed. She came into my room and helped me put my dress on. I put eye liner and lip stick on and then his mother helped me put on my veil. I looked in my dressing mirror and felt so beautiful. I was so happy. The door bell rang and Sherry went to get the door. She came into the room and told me that the limo had arrived. We got into the limo and the driver headed to the church. As we drove to the church my life flashed before me. I thought of all I had been through and the first day I met Thomas. I smiled. Thomas' mother asked what I was thinking about. I told her that I was thinking about when I first met Thomas. We really didn't say that we were dating, we were just having fun. We grew up together, broke up and went in different directions, but we never forgot each other and became friends. She hugged me and said that she was so happy that Thomas and I were getting married. When we got to the church the limo parked. The driver got out and opened the door. Thomas' mother got out the car and went into the church. Within five minutes two grooms men came out of the church. They helped my bridesmaids out of the limo and walked into the church.

After they disappeared Thomas' father came out of the church. He put his hand out. I took it and got out of the limo. I was so nervous. I put my arm in his. He placed his other hand on my arm. We began our walk. When we walked into the church everyone stood up. The music began playing and the singer started singing "You and I." Mr. Stone and I began walking towards the front of the church. As I kept my eyes on Thomas I thought of my mother. I thought how it would have been great if she was here with me. All of a sudden I felt a chill. Mr. Stone noticed and asked me if I was alright. I told him that I was. I said inside my head, "Is that you momma?" We continued to progress to the front of the church. When we got to the front of the church Thomas came to meet me. Mr. Stone took my arm from around his and placed it in Thomas' arm.

Thomas and I walked to the minister. The minister said, "We are gathered here today to witness these two people who are in love with each other so much that they have come to ask God to make them one in spirit. They have written their own vows." The minister looked at Thomas and said Thomas recite your vows.

Thomas looked at me and began, "***Monic Renee Coldwater you are an inspiration to me. You're kind, generous, intelligent and most of all loving. I thought I lost you once, but fate brought us back together. I feel blessed that God brought you to me. I promise to always value all that you do and to be there to support you. I'll always love you, cherish you and keep you, until death do us part.***"

The minister turned to me and said Monic. I began, "***Thomas Edward Stone Jr. you have been my friend, my confidant, the love of my life and my rock. I will love you forever. I promise to cherish every moment of our lives together and be the wife that you want, need and deserve. I promise to always be here for you.***"

The minister said the rings please. We repeated what the minister said and placed the rings on each others fingers.

The minister went on, "We have heard from Thomas and Monic, if there is anyone who for any reason know why these two should not be wed, speak now or forever hold your peace." The minister waited a few minutes and then began again. He said, "God has brought these two together and let no one pull them apart. Thomas and Monic I pronounce you husband and wife. Thomas you may now kiss your bride." Thomas took me in his arms and kissed me with such a sensual kiss that I forgot where I was. Thomas stopped abruptly and everyone laughed.

The minister said, "I present Mr. and Mrs. Thomas Edward Stone Jr." Everyone stood up and clapped. Thomas took my hand and we walked out of the church and into the limo. When we were out of site Thomas pulled me close and began to kiss me. He caressed the side of my face and said you are so beautiful. He told me that it took all of his strength not to pull me to him in church. I smiled. We kissed and then he caressed and kissed parts of my body that was exposed all the way to the hall. My body craved for more. When we arrived in front of the reception hall the driver parked and got out of the car. I fixed myself before he opened the door. When he opened the car door Thomas got out first and then held his hand out to me. I took it and got out of the limo. We walked hand in hand into the hall. We were escorted up to the holding room. Soon after the bridle party came in. We mingled with the bridle party for a little while and then we went down to the reception. They announced everyone and each couple walked in as they called their names.

When they called our names we walked into the room. Everyone stood up and clapped. Music began to play. Thomas and I had our first dance as man and wife. He held me close and we swayed to the music. Thomas whispered that he loved me and nibbled on my ear. We continued to sway even after the music stopped. The DJ said ok you two the music has stopped. Everyone laughed and we took our seats. As the food was served soft music played. We ate and occasionally Thomas fed me. After we were finished eating dinner Thomas and I walked around the room. We walked around thanking each person for attending. Shortly after returning to our table it was time to throw the bouquet. I got up and walked to the middle of the floor. The single women stood opposite me. The DJ played music. I turned around and then the DJ began to count. On three I threw the bouquet in the air. The women scattered to scattered to catch it. After catching it the DJ announced that it was time for Thomas to throw my garter. A chair was brought to the middle of the floor. I sat in it. The DJ changed the music and then Thomas danced over to me. He got on the floor and crawled on his knees. He did not use his hands. I raised my dress. Thomas put his mouth on my garter and began moving it down my leg. When it was down my leg Thomas placed his hand on my foot and removed the garter. He kissed me tenderly and then stood up. The DJ instructed the single men to come to the floor. They hesitantly got up and stood behind Thomas. The DJ continued to play music and the began to count. On ten Thomas turned his back to the group of men. He threw the garter up and the air and the men stood back. The garter hit the floor. Then one brave man picked it up. The lady that caught the bouquet was instructed to sit in the chair that I had sat in. She did as instructed. The DJ instructed the man with the garter to place it on her leg. The man placed it on the woman's leg. Everyone clapped. After a few songs played, we then went over to cut the cake. Thomas and I hand in hand cut the cake. He took a small amount and fed me a piece. I in turn fed him. Afterwards we kissed.

It was finally time for us to take our leave. Mrs. Stone volunteered to hold onto the gifts that people brought. I thanked her again for all that she had done to help this day be wonderful and then Thomas and I left. We changed and then got back into the limo. The driver drove us to the airport. We checked in and headed for the gate. Once we arrived at the gate Thomas and I sat down. I layed my head on Thomas' chest and closed my eyes.

CHAPTER 12

The Honey Moon

It wasn't long before the airline began calling for first class to board. I sat up and then Thomas and I got up to board the plane. We took our seats. I strapped in and leaned back. Within a few minutes I fell asleep. When I awakened the flight attendants were bringing our meal. Thomas was still sleeping so I took his meal. I couldn't believe how great it was in first class. Well I didn't know anything else, I had never been in a plane before. It felt exciting. I had begun eating my meal when Thomas woke up. He saw that I had gotten his meal. He smiled and said so you're already looking out for me. I told him always. He leaned over, lightly kissed me and said thank you. We ate and watched the movie that was playing. After eating we both drifted off to sleep. After several hours of going in and out of sleep our flight landed in Australia. We were taken to the hotel. We entered the lobby of Observatory Hotel in Sydney. The lobby was unbelievably beautiful and spacious. The flowers in the entry way were breath taking. We checked in and was taken to our room. Thomas picked me up and carried me into the room. We looked around the room. It was beautiful. We showered together. Thomas and I took turns washing each other. With each of Thomas' touches I felt tingles. Washing him made my body long for him even more. I couldn't believe that spending just one week away from him could make me miss him so much. We kissed and caressed each other's body. After some time Thomas turned off the water. He dried himself off and then me. He picked me up, carried me to the bed and then layed me down. He layed next to me and began kissing me. He caressed my body until I couldn't take it. I called out his name. He looked up at me and smiled. I pulled the covers back. We began to kiss. Thomas laid on top of me and we moved in unison. It felt so good being so close. Thomas held me in his strong muscular arms. I held onto them as our passion rose to heights unimaginable. As we moved together I kissed his chest. His sweat was sweet. I thought how much I loved him. I held him as tight as I could. I wanted us to be as close as we could get. I clung to him until our love making reached it's peak. We kissed passionately and soon drifted off to sleep still mesh together as one.

When we awakened our passions rose again. After hours of love making and resting we went out to eat. We dined in the Galileo Restaurant. It was so wonderful. When we were done eating we returned to our room. Thomas and I drank the Champagne that had been left for us. We gazed out onto the beauty of the view. We snacked on the fruit that was in the room. We then layed on the chase and began watching a movie on the television. Thomas caressed my shoulders and then began kissing them. He turned the movie down and we made love into the night.

The next day we awakened and went down to have breakfast. After breakfast we went out onto the grounds and walked hand in hand. Then Thomas placed his arm around my shoulders. We stopped and took pictures of the scenery. Thomas placed his arms around my waist and we kissed. A passerby saw the camera in my hands and interrupted the kiss. He offered to take a picture of us. Thomas continued to hold me close while the man took our picture. Afterwards we continued touring the grounds. We were out there for several hours. We finally returned to our room. We changed into our swim suits and went down to the pool. Thomas and I played and splashed around the pool. He was such a good swimmer. We had never gone swimming together before, so watching him was exciting. I got out of the pool and laid on one of the lounge chairs next to the pool. I continued watching Thomas swim. We stayed in the pool for a while. I could see that he loved the water. I thought it amazing that I didn't know this Thomas and how even though we had known each other a long time there would be other things that I did not know about this man. When he finally got out of the pool we decided to get a light lunch.

Thomas and I went back to our room and layed down. I was surprised when he rolled onto his side and asked me when did I want to begin having children. I thought for a minute and then told him that I was ready whenever he was. He told me that he wanted to start a family right away. I told him that when we returned home that I would go to the doctor and have him remove the item inside of me that I was using for birth control. This seemed to please him. We stayed in our room the rest of the night and ordered in. The next day we went on a tour. Everywhere we went was unbelievably beautiful that I thought I died and went to heaven. After the tour Thomas and I decided to eat before returning to the hotel. When we returned to our hotel room we ordered fruit and was given more champagne. We turned the television on and watched a show and snacked on our fruit and drank the champagne. As it got late Thomas got hungry. The fruit wasn't enough. We decided to down to the hotel restaurant and ate a light meal. We then went for a walk around the grounds. It was so beautiful at night. The lights from the Resort made it seem light we were dreaming. It was so beautiful that we hated that it was our last night.

The next day we went to Lizard Island, Great Barrier Reef. We stayed there two days. The mountains were breath taking. The rooms there were equally romantic. We went site seeing. I took a lot of pictures. I wanted to capture all of it's beauty. I had never been surrounded by so much beauty. When we returned to our hotel room Thomas and I changed into swim suits and went to the indoor swimming pool. The pool was enormous. When I stepped into the pool I couldn't believe how good it felt. It was warm and soothing to the skin. Although we did some swimming I enjoyed laying beside the pool. I enjoyed watching the designs reflecting off of the pool against the walls. One of the couples staying in the hotel told us about a club near by.

After leaving the pool Thomas and I took a nap. When we woke up a few hours later Thomas and I took a shower together and dressed to go to the club. When we arrived there the couple was there. They motioned to us to share their table. We watched the others in the club dancing. We had a few drinks and talked to the couple for a while. When one they finally played a familiar song Thomas asked me to dance. I got up and we danced all night. When the club closed Thomas and I walked down the lit up street to our hotel. Although the club was different than what we were use to we rather enjoyed ourselves. We took a quick shower and went to bed.

The next morning we aroused early and quickly dressed. We packed our things and then left our room. There was a car waiting for us. We got into the car and it took us to the airport. I was exhausted. As soon as we entered the plane I fell asleep. I slept throughout the flight. When it was time to return home I had mixed feelings. I wanted us to remain the way we were. During our ride back home we discussed starting our family. Thomas said that he wanted four children. I voiced my concerns. I wanted to have children with my husband, but I have concerns about being a good mother and I worry about me being abused.

Dr. Gordan said, "Is that what brought you here?"

"Yes. I worry about me being a good mother."

"Do you want children or are you thinking about having children because Thomas wants them?"

"I have thought about having children. When I held Terrance Jr. I thought how innocent he was and how wondered if I would have any. I thought how wonderful it would be for Thomas and I to have a son, but then I think about the abuse that I grew up with. I think about all the secrets I kept. I think of all the secrets that my mother never told me. I often wondered did she know to tell me."

"So you worry that you might be an abuser?"

"Yes."

"In your sessions you talked of children in the house. Did you ever feel anything that wasn't natural, or that was inappropriate?"

(Monic thought a few minutes) "Other than wanting them to grow up normal, no. (Monic smiled) "No I didn't have any lustful feelings towards them."

"That's your answer."

"Thank you doctor."

"For what? I don't think that you need to make another appointment. If you feel that you need to come back, don't hesitate." The two got up. Monic shook Dr. Gordon's hand. Dr. Gordon said, "Have a good life."

"I'll do my best."

CHAPTER 13

The Beginning of a New Life

Monic returned to her apartment. She continued to pack her things to be moved into their new home. It had been two weeks since their honeymoon. They had moved most of their things into their new house. Monic had an appointment with her Gynecologist. Monic explained to the doctor that she and Thomas had talked about starting a family. Doctor Brown ran test and everything proved normal. Two weeks later Monic got home early. She prepared a romantic dinner. As the time approached for Thomas to come home she showered and put on a dress that was flattering to her figure. She sprayed perfume on delicate points of her body. When the door opened she met Thomas and greeted him with a sensuous kiss.

He held her to him and said, "What's this?"

"I missed you."

"Really?"

"Yes."

Thomas held her tighter. Monic gently pulled away and took him by the hand. "I made us a romantic dinner."

Thomas said, "Wow, what did I do or should I ask what did you do?"

"I just thought it would be nice. We've been so busy and haven't really spent any time together, other than getting the house together."

Thomas followed her into the dinning room. The table was set. Monic had placed their crystal flutes and fine china out. Two crystal candles were lit and placed on either side of the table. Champagne was chilling at one end of the table. Rose peddles were lightly sprinkled on the table. Monic turned on soft music.

Thomas said, "What is all this?"

"I just wanted to make things romantic."

Thomas looked at Monic suspiciously. Monic placed the food on the table. They fixed their plates. As the two ate Thomas continued to look at Monic in a suspicious manner. After the meal Monic got up, walked over to Thomas and put her hand out. Thomas took it. She picked up the bottle. Monic pointed to the glasses and said, "Get those." Thomas obeyed.

They went into the family room. Monic placed the bottle down. Thomas said, "May I have this dance?"

Monic went into his arms. She thought how much she loved to dance and Thomas was such a good dancer. Lost in the ambiance and music they danced for a while. Prior to Thomas coming home Monic had dimmed the lights and lit candles through out the house. Thomas lightly caressed Monic's body as they danced, sending shivers through her. Monic rested her head against Thomas chest and he caressed it. Monic looked up at Thomas in such a loving way he stopped dancing.

He said, "You take my heart when you look at me like that."

"What do you mean? How am I looking at you?"

"It's hard to explain. It's just the way you look at me. Make me feel honored that someone loves me so much."

"I do love you with all of my heart. I love you more than words can express."

"I love you too."

"I know. Thomas do you really want to have a family with me?"

At first Thomas thought how silly the question was, but looking at Monic, he saw in her expression an uncertainty. He took her by the hand and said, "I would love to have a family with you. You are so beautiful and smart I know we'll have good looking intelligent kids. Is that what all the seduction is about?"

Monic looked embarrassed. Thomas picked her up into his arms and carried her up to their bedroom. He layed her onto the bed. He looked at her and said, "So you're ready to start a family?"

"I'm getting older and I don't want to wait to long. I want to be able to enjoy our babies while I'm still young."

"So you want a girl or boy first?"

Monic smiled and said, "I would like a boy. I want to give you a son. What would you like?"

"A son sounds good, but I would love to have a beautiful little girl to look as gorgeous as her mother."

"Well I would like to give you a daughter first."

"Then it's settled?"

"What?"

"Our first born being a girl."

"What you're going to will it?"

"I have a technique."

"Oh really?"

With that Thomas turned the music station. He began to dance seductively. As he danced he removed his clothes. He watched Monic. He moved in closer to her. While still dancing erotically he removed her clothes. He changed the speed of the music. He pulled her to stand up. Thomas pulled her into him and they began to dance. Monic couldn't believe how all of this was turning her on. As they moved together Monic caressed Thomas' body. They continued their erotic dance until their bodies called for completion....

Two months later Monic became concerned. She thought for sure she would be pregnant. She went back to the doctor. The doctor explained to her how birth control worked. He told her not to worry. Monic was still concerned that she would fail in giving Thomas children. When Monic arrived home she smelled food and heard music. She went into the kitchen and saw Thomas preparing dinner. When she entered the room Thomas looked up and smiled.

"What are you doing home?"

"Well I thought it would be nice to come home and brighten up your day. You seem stressed lately. You're not worried about getting pregnant are you?"

"A little."

Thomas left what he was doing and walked over to her. He pulled her towards him. He backed up pulling her closer to him. As he leaned against the counter he said,

"Don't worry so much. It will come. Soon we're going to be running around here chasing babies."

"I hope you're right."

"What did the doctor say?"

"He said that my birth control has to get out of my system."

"Then it's settled. When it's time you'll get pregnant. Let's enjoy us for now."

"I'm sorry."

"For what?"

"Acting like this."

"You have nothing to be sorry for. I love you and if something is bothering you I'm concerned. Come over here and sit down. I'm going to serve you tonight."

Thomas went back to preparing dinner. He fixed their plates. They ate. Thomas had purchased a Black Forest Cake. He cut one slice and put it on a plate. He took out one fork. Thomas took Monic by the hand and led her up to their bedroom. Rose peddles were on and around the bed. Thomas sat the plate of cake down. He undressed Monic, leaving only her lingerie on. He removed his clothes. Thomas took Monic into the bathroom where the Jacuzzi was filled with water and more rose peddles. Thomas helped her into the tub. He went over and picked up the plate and brought it into the bathroom. He then entered the Jacuzzi. Thomas moved close to Monic. He began to feed the cake to her. He in turn ate some of it. Thomas filled one crystal flute with champagne. He sipped it and then gave Monic some. They finished off the slice of cake and continued to share the flute. Thomas told Monic about his childhood. They laughed at his various stories. Thomas noticed that Monic was relaxing.

He could actually see it in her posture. Thomas had never seen her this way. He commented on it. Monic thought about it and admitted that she had never felt this way before.

She said, "While I was listening to you I could actually visualize you as a little boy. I envisioned you and your sisters playing in the yard with no care in the world. You must have been so happy. For the first time I thought of our children playing in the yard. I thought of how wonderful a father you will be."

That night Thomas made love to his new wife. She was no longer the little girl he had met so many years ago. She was no longer the exploring teenager trying to act grown up, nor was she the young woman that he had reacquainted himself with and married. Monic had grown up to this mature woman, no longer afraid of herself. She had conquered her demons and let go of all the bad things that she had gone through. This woman he would spend his life with and raise their children.

CHAPTER 14

The Beginning of a New Life

A month later Monic began feeling tired. Monic began taking naps when she arrived home from work. After doing this for a month Monic began taking vitamins. She thought that she was coming down with something. When she missed her menstruation two consecutive months Monic bought a pregnancy test on her way into work. Before she began work she went into the bathroom and took the pregnancy test. She waited anxiously for the test results. It came back positive. She called her doctor and scheduled an appointment. She left work early and headed to the doctor's office.

When Monic arrived at the doctor she checked in with the receptionist. Monic waited excitedly to see the doctor. When her name was called she hurried to the nurse. After running various test the doctor came back into the office and informed her that she was pregnant. Monic just sat there for a moment to collect her thoughts. She couldn't believe what she was hearing. The doctor asked her if she was alright. Monic nodded yes. The doctor gave her a prescription for prenatal vitamins. She scheduled an appointment to return in two months. Monic proudly took her prescription and headed to her car.

When she got into her car she kissed the prescription. Monic started the car and headed to the drug store. She dropped the prescription off and decided to go to the grocery store while the prescription was being filled. Monic picked up healthy foods and snacks. She wanted a healthy pregnancy and baby. She didn't want anything to jeopardize it. Monic also picked up food to make a special dinner for her and Thomas.

When Monic was finished shopping she returned to the drug store. She picked up her prescription and then returned to her car. Monic was so excited that she opened juice that she had left out from grocery shopping, opened the vitamin bottle and took one. Then she drove off and headed home. When she arrived home Monic put up the grocery. She left out what she was going to cook for dinner that night. Monic went up to her room and laid down. When she awakened Monic smelled food. She looked at the clock and jumped up. It was six o'clock. Monic went down to the kitchen. When she entered the kitchen Monic saw Thomas. He had cooked dinner. He had taken plates out of the cupboard and placed them on trays.

When he heard Monic enter the kitchen Thomas looked up. "I was just about to bring you dinner."

"I'm sorry. I planned to fix dinner for us."

"I called your job and they said that you left early. When I came home and saw you sleeping I figured you weren't feeling well. Are you alright?"

"I'm fine."

"Are you sure? You seem sluggish. Are you sick? You should go to the doctor."

Monic walked over to Thomas and kissed him. She took his hand and lead him to sit down. After he sat down Monic sat on his lap. Thomas said, "What's wrong?"

Monic replied, "Nothing. I have something to tell you."

Thomas got a worried look on his face. Monic kissed him again. With a smile on her face Monic said, "We're going to have a baby."

Thomas looked at her in disbelief. "Are you sure?"

"Yes. I took a pregnancy test at work and then I left work early today, went to the doctor and he confirmed it."

"Baby are you feeling alright?"

"I'm fine. The doctor prescribed prenatal vitamins."

Thomas touched Monic's stomach, rubbed it and said," Hey in there. I'm daddy." He pick Monic up and carried her up to their bedroom. He sat her on the bed. Thomas returned to the kitchen and got their food. He brought it upstairs. The couple ate and discussed their plans for the new addition. Monic and Thomas agreed not to tell anyone about the pregnancy until she was five months or showing. Monic didn't want to tell anyone because she was still nervous about carrying to full term. She remembered when she was pregnant. How for many months she thought that she was sick and going to die. She didn't know that she was pregnant. When something in her began to move she went to her husband. He looked at her and said, "Don't you know because you weren't careful you have a baby inside of you." Still too young to comprehend fear came over her and she felt like she had done something wrong to her husband. Thomas called her, then gently touched her, bringing her back to the present.

He said, "Hey are you alright?"

"I'm fine. I was just thinking about my past. My first pregnancy."

"Things are different. You are a woman now. That was a little girl who didn't have a clue to what was going on and what to do. You will be fine. Things are going to be great. I love you Monic."

Thomas put his arms around Monic and pulled her close to him. They held each other, not saying anything else. The couple drifted off to sleep. Thomas woke up in the middle of the night. He took off his clothes. Thomas eased back into the bed and took Monic into his arms. Monic nestled her head on his chest. The next morning Monic awakened. She was still in Thomas' arms. She layed there a little while before getting up. Monic thought of how happy she was. She couldn't believe how happy she was with this husband. She felt secure. Monic thought how blessed she was to have a husband such as Thomas and now she was going to have a beautiful baby with him. She kissed him lightly on the lips and then got up. She got ready for work. Once she was dressed Monic walked over to the bed. She bent down and kissed Thomas. He put his arms around her and pulled her onto him. They kissed and then Thomas let her up. He said, "Have a good day."

Monic went into the office. She couldn't believe how good she felt. During the morning Monic caught herself rubbing her stomach. When she would catch herself

Monic would look down at her stomach and smile. At lunch time her telephone rang. She picked it up. The receptionist told her that she had a lunch date. Monic told her to send them in. Monic was surprised when the door opened. It was Thomas.

Monic said, "What are you doing here?"

"I got a few hours in between cases so I decided to take my beautiful wife out so she can feed my baby."

"You must have sensed we were getting hungry."

The couple left the office. Thomas took Monic to a restaurant that was not far from her job. The couple ate and talked. After they had finished their meal Thomas took Monic back to her office. He walked her in. He kissed her and left.

Monic tried to concentrate, but her mind drifted to her first pregnancy. She tried to remember how she felt. She could only remember the fear of something being inside her. Monic thought of the horror movies that she watched when she was small. She thought maybe one of the aliens had come down and put something inside her. That one day it was going to burst out of her and she would die. Monic thought how naive she was even though she was having sex. Her husband taught her how to be clean. He never explained sex to her or what they were doing. She was thankful that he never tried to have her do the things that he had the other girls do. She wondered now, "If he really did love her. If in fact he really wanted to be a father to her. Why did he bring the other girls there and leave her to grow up and experience life the way children are suppose to." Although she had to come home and see what was going on in the house she was able to come into her own. She was able to go out with kids her own age and even though he didn't know it, she had boyfriends. Monic thought to herself, "I actually enjoyed my life outside of my house." She thought how awful a price the other girls paid to give her the life she is enjoying now. Monic walked over to her office door, locked it and then kneeled down to pray. As she prayed tears streamed down her face. Although these girls who were either not much older than her, or younger than herself, those who she knew and the ones that she hoped that may have avoid the life of abuse. She thought of them as her surrogate mothers and because of their ages her sisters. She mourned for their lost of innocence, their peace and their lives. She mourned for not getting closer to them because of their situation. Monic prayed for all her sisters/mothers, for those young girls out in the world still being subjected to abuse (whether physical and or mental) she said a prayer for her biological mother, for her husband, her marriage and her unborn child. After she was finished Monic got off her knees, went over to her desk and looked in the mirror to make sure there was no sign that there had been tears in her eyes. She unlocked her office door and then sat down. Monic saw clients the rest of the day.

For the next few months everything was going along smoothly. At seven months Thomas and Monic chose the baby's room. They decorated it on the weekends. Monic had not told anyone on the job. She had not begun to show.

As the months past Monic began getting excited about her pregnancy. She was amazed at how Thomas looked forward to the baby's arrival. Monic loved the way Thomas would lay his head on her stomach and talk to the baby. She thought it interesting how the baby moving take his love to a higher level if that's possible. In her eighth month she informed her job. Everyone was excited for her....

A week before Monic was going on maternity leave the job threw her a baby shower. Her sister-in-laws also threw her a shower the week before she was due. Monic put up all the gifts that she had been given.

Monic and Thomas searched for books to read to the baby. Thomas built a book shelf to place the baby books. At night Monic would read the books, aloud, Thomas would rest his head on her lap and listened. Sometimes Thomas would read. Three days before Monic's due date she became restless. Monic would go into the baby's room to make sure everything was ready for the baby. She sat down in the rocking chair. She drifted off to sleep.

Monic began to dream: "She was ten years old. She had begun having contractions. They hurt so bad. She thought that she was dieing. Monic called out to her mother, but she did not come. Monic began to cry. She was afraid. Then her water broke. The pressure was intense and she didn't know what to do. She remembered the alien movies and thought it was finally coming. As she cried calling out for her mother Monic heard her name." Monic woke up. Thomas was standing over her.

"Monic. Are you okay?"

Monic wasn't sure of where she was and just stared at him. Thomas realized that her water had broke. He said, "Monic it's Thomas. Baby your water broke."

Monic realized where she was and jumped up. She looked at herself. "I have to clean myself up."

"Do you have time?"

"Yes. I won't take long. Call the hospital."

Thomas called the hospital. Monic's doctor was on call. Thomas grabbed Monic's bag. Monic was ready and they left for the hospital. As they drove the contractions were getting closer. By the time they reached the hospital Monic was ready to deliver. They immediately wheeled her to the maternity ward. The doctor examined her and she was taken to the birthing room. A hour later the couple was given to hold a baby girl. Monic held her baby girl and kissed her. Thomas' eyes filled with tears. He kissed them both. Monic was cleaned up and taken to her room.

Once the couple was alone Thomas said, "You did it. Thank you."

"Thomas thank you for being so wonderful."

Thomas kissed Monic on the lips. The nurse entered the room with the baby. After the nurse left Thomas picked up the baby and kissed her. He then brought her over to Monic. He said, "I think she's hungry. Monic took the baby and held her close. She opened her blouse. Thomas looked on in amazement. After the baby had gotten full she fell asleep. Monic looked up at Thomas wanting him to be a part of the moment, she asked, "Would you like to burp her?"

Thomas took the baby and rubbed her back. After the baby had burped Thomas continued to hold her. Monic looked at her husband and felt such love. She knew he would be a good father. The baby was named after the two grandmothers, Tyler from Monic's mother and Marie after Thomas' mother.

The next day mother and baby were released from the hospital. Thomas had taken maternity leave from his job, the week that she was due. Although Monic breast feed most of the time, she also pumped so Thomas could feed the baby and she could get some rest. Thomas' family came by a few times after Monic came home. They made their visit short because they realized that the couple weren't up for visits. Thomas and Monic seemed to close the world out. Thomas would sometimes watch as Monic breast fed the baby. When the baby slept Thomas and Monic spent time together. Monic enjoyed these moments. Thomas held her at night and before she would fall asleep he'd whisper "I love you."

During the time Thomas feed Tyler he would tell her, "I'm going to always be here for you and your mother." Tyler would smile as if she knew what her father was saying.

Six months past. Thomas returned to work. Although Monic missed Thomas she enjoyed the moments she had alone with Tyler.

During these moments she thought about her life experience. Monic decided that she wanted to do something with children. Monic decided to resign from her job and open up a clinic for abuse and exploited children. She discussed it with Thomas and he thought it was a good idea....

It was approaching Tyler's birthday. They threw Tyler a birthday party. During the party Thomas' mother asked "When is Monic returning to work? I can baby sit."

"Mom, Monic resigned."

"What" You didn't say anything."

"She decided that she wanted to do something else."

"What?"

"She's researching working with problem children."

"Can't she do that at her job?"

"She wants to work exclusively with children. I can't

tell you any more than that. She will say more when she have everything worked out."

"Can you guys afford her not working?"

"We're fine mom."

Just then Monic walked into the kitchen. Thomas' mother said, "So I hear you're not returning to your job."

"Yes. I can't explain it, but I want to do something else."

"You can't figure things out while you're working? I mean can you two afford for you not to work?"

Thomas said, "Mom, I told you we are fine."

"Yes right now. Monic are you sure you are not just afraid to leave the baby?"

"Yes I'm sure. I understand what you're saying. "Thomas looked at Monic and was surprised to see that she was calm. He didn't see any irritation in her face when she spoke with his mother. Monic continued, "I know you're concerned. Please know that I would never do anything to jeopardize the security or happiness of my family. Being home with my daughter, having this time to think lead me to believe that I could do more for people. There are so many messed up people in the world." Thomas looked on. He did not only love his wife, he admired her strength and determination. Monic went on to say, "I just want to give back. Thomas, Tyler and I will always be fine and how many other children we may have. Don't worry I know what I'm doing."

Thomas father put his harm around his wife and said, "Honey the children know what they're doing. Monic we are here if you need us."

Thomas' mother looked at him and then said, "Well I guess you two have made up your mind. Good luck."

After the party Thomas and Monic cleaned up. The couple put Tyler to bed and Thomas read her a story. Monic and Thomas went into their room. They got into bed. Thomas held Monic. He said, "I was so proud of you today. You are an exceptional beautiful woman."

Monic looked at him and said, "Do you really understand what I want to do?"

"Yes and I understand why."

"You are such a good husband."

"I try."

"Thomas."

"Yes."

"When would you like to have another baby?"

Thomas adjusted himself. He looked at Monic. He asked, "What are you saying?"

"No I'm not pregnant. I wanted to know because I would have to come off the birth control depending on when you wanted another child."

"Are you ready? I mean whenever you're ready."

"I'm ready. Tyler is one and I would like her to be close to her sibling."

"We can begin tonight."

Thomas pulled Monic to him. He began kissing her. He stopped and said, "By the way, how many do you want?"

"Four."

"Well I better get busy"…..

Three months later Monic was pregnant. When she told Thomas he decided that they should add on to their home. While the house was large enough for another child or two he recalled their conversation about having four. He talked with a contractor. The two sat with Monic and went over what Thomas wanted done to the house. They added two additional bedrooms, expanded the family room, the kitchen and made a recreational room in the basement. They created a playroom in the basement and moved the adult entertainment area that had been build prior to them moving there. The children's room spilled out into the backyard. While Thomas concentrated on the renovations Monic surveyed areas for her clinic. She found a lot that had been vacant for several years. It was on a bus route. Monic was able to purchase it for a very low cost. She bought it out right thinking economically it would be less costly not paying on time. With Thomas' help Monic drew a floor plan. They used the same contracting company that was used for their home. Monic oversaw the construction. During the construction Monic interviewed and hired the staff. She partnered with local and government businesses for donations and prospective clients. Monic and Thomas decided to name the building The C.C.Care Center For Abuse and Exploited Children. The name was derived from Cynthia who committed suicide and Carry who also killed Tracy, her two babies, Monic's father and herself. The building would house ten family's, had a nursery for abandoned children, that could house 15, a counseling facility and recreation room for teens to young adults. Monic used money from her father's death benefits, donations from local businesses and the community. She was also able to qualify for some grants from the federal government. The doors would open up in a year.

Monic's pregnancy was going smoothly. The

construction of their home was completed by her seventh month. Thomas accompanied Monic to her seventh month doctor's appointment. During the visit they discovered that Monic was pregnant with twins. They were excited, but didn't want to know the sex. After leaving the doctor's office the couple went shopping for cribs. Although it was tempting, the couple decided not to buy, everything identical, Tyler was excited about her new siblings. They decided to use the two bedrooms next to Tyler's room.

Monic had to slow down in her eighth month. Thomas took maternity leave when Monic went into her ninth month. When Monic went into labor Thomas' mother came to the hospital to take care of Tyler. Tyler fell asleep after the first hour of Monic's labor. Three and a half hours later Monic gave birth to twin boys. Tyler was brought into the delivery room. She smiled as she looked at her baby brothers. Two days later mother and babies were released from the hospital. When Monic entered the house Tyler ran up and hugged her. She said, "Mommy, Daddy, you're back."

Monic said, "You missed mommy and daddy?"

"Yes. Grandmom said you'll be home soon. You took a long time."

"We did? Well we missed you too. Did you have a good time with grandmom and granddad?"

"Yes."

Monic and Thomas took the babies to their rooms. While the babies were asleep they spent time with Tyler. Monic thanked Thomas' mother and she left. A few hours later Monic laid down. Thomas took Tyler to her room and read her a book. He prepared her for bed. When he went back in his bedroom Monic was awake. She was going towards the door.

Thomas asked, "Did you rest well?"

"Yes."

"Where are you going? The babies are still asleep and Tyler is fast asleep."

"Thank you for putting her to bed."

"No need to thank me, that's my baby girl too. Where are you going?"

"The babies should be waking up."

When they entered the first baby's room whose named was Malcolm they saw that he was awake. He was laying quietly. Monic picked him up. She sat in the rocker and positioned the baby to feed him. After he had gotten enough Thomas took him to burp and change his diaper. Monic went into the second baby's room Thomas Jr. He was just waking up and was moving around. Monic picked him up and then walked back into Malcolm's room. She sat in the rocker. She breast fed Thomas Jr. She watched Thomas as he played with Malcolm. They stayed in Malcolm's room for a while. After putting the babies to bed Thomas and Monic returned to their bedroom. Monic laid in Thomas arms. She soon drifted off to sleep. Thomas laid Monic's head gently on her pillow and then eased out of bed. Thomas went through the house checking the children's rooms. He then went down to the family room and put in a movie. He fell asleep. Thomas kept this routine for a month. One night Monic woke up at three a.m. She did not see Thomas. She checked on the babies. Malcolm was awake. She fed him. She went to Thomas Jr.'s room. He was still asleep. Monic went to check on Tyler. She fixed her covers and left the room.

Monic went downstairs. She surveyed the area. The next place she looked was the family room. Thomas was sitting in his favorite chair asleep. Monic gently sat in his lap. She gently kissed his lips. After a few times he put his arms around her waist and returned her affections. Monic could tell that he missed this. They had been so busy with the children they had very little time alone.

The next morning Thomas and Monic awakened at seven o'clock. They were still in the family room. They could hear Thomas Jr. crying. Thomas went up to feed him while Monic took a shower. When she came out of the shower she could hear Malcolm crying. She put on a robe and walked towards his room to feed him. When she entered his room Thomas was in there feeding Thomas Jr. Monic was kind of tired so she picked up Malcolm and walked by to her bedroom. She laid in the bed and fed him. After some time Monic fell asleep. Thomas laid Thomas Jr. down and then came into their bedroom. He saw that Monic and Malcolm was asleep. He eased Malcolm from Monic and took him into his room. Thomas checked his diaper and then changed him. Thomas placed him in the bed and returned to the bedroom. When he returned to the room Tyler was standing in the doorway.

She said, "Good morning daddy."

Thomas picked her up and replied, "Hi Princess. Are you hungry?"

"Yes daddy."

"Ok let's get you dressed and then I'll fix breakfast."

"Daddy can I help?"

"Yes you may."

Tyler hugged Thomas and said, "Thank you daddy."

Thomas took Tyler into her room. He turned on the

shower. After giving her a shower Thomas wrapped Tyler in a towel. He found clothes for her to wear. Once she was dressed they went downstairs to the kitchen. Thomas gave Tyler a few cereal while she waited for him to prepare breakfast. When breakfast was done Thomas fixed plates for Tyler, Monic and himself. He placed them on a tray. Thomas carried the tray in one hand and helped Tyler with the other. He and Tyler entered his bedroom. Tyler got ready to run and Thomas stopped her.

He said, "Quietly."

As they walked over to the bed Monic woke up. She shifted in the bed. Tyler ran over. "Mommy we fixed you breakfast."

Monic sat up. She smiled and said, "Aren't you wonderful?" Tyler put her arms around Monic's neck. Monic gave her a warm hug.

Thomas said, "Do I get one of those too?"

With a mischievous look Monic said, "I think you got yours earlier. But I think you deserve another."

Thomas bent down and kissed Monic. The three positioned themselves in the bed and began eating. After eating Thomas and Tyler went downstairs. Tyler practiced her numbers and alphabets as Thomas cleaned the kitchen. Monic pumped her breast. When she was done Monic brought the milk down to the kitchen and put it in the freezer. Monic then went back upstairs. One at a time she gave the babies a bath. Monic cleaned their rooms and went to the family room. As she came into the room Thomas looked up. He gave her a devious grin. Monic sat next to Tyler and watched her play.

A month later Monic began preparing for the opening of the C.C. Care Center. She felt sluggish. Thomas noticed and asked "Are you coming down with something? Do you need to eat more?"

Monic responded, "No. Maybe feeding two babies is taking a lot out of me."

Thomas cautiously said, "Well maybe you need to postpone the opening of the center."

"I'll be alright."

"Baby I don't want you getting sick."

"I won't."

Thomas turned around. "Do you think that you're pregnant?"

"No. I'm back on birth control."

"Oh."

For the next month Thomas did more around the house to let Monic rest. He still didn't see any improvement in Monic's health. Monic was getting worried as well. She was resting as much as possible. Monic tried to pump as much as possible so Thomas could feed the babies more, so she could rest. Monic decided to go to the doctor. She made an appointment. Thomas had his mother watch the children while he and Monic went to the doctor. When they got to the doctor Monic signed in. After a few minutes she was called. Monic and Thomas followed the nurse. Monic's vitals were taken. When the doctor came in he ordered blood work and asked Monic to submit urine. He asked her questions. Monic left the room to give urine. When she returned the doctor hooked up the baby monitor. As he moved the mouse he saw a figure. The doctor went over it again. Monic glanced at the doctor. After seeing the expression on his face Monic asked, "What is it?"

The doctor did not say anything at first. He continued

to move the mouse. The doctor looked at Monic. He enlarged the picture. The doctor said, "Monic when did you go back on birth control?"

"Last month. Why?"

"You're pregnant."

Just then the nurse came into the room. The doctor looked at the results. The doctor turned to Monic and Thomas again. "You are pregnant."

Monic said, "I don't understand. I'm on birth control."

The doctor said, "Did you have unprotected sex at any time?"

Monic thought about it and just when she began to speck Thomas said, "When did you come to the family room? Wasn't that two months ago?"

Monic thought about it and in a low tone said, "Yes."

The doctor commented, "Are you ready for more good news? Monic looked at him You're having twins. The doctor smiled. "I guess you'll be visiting the family room more often."

Monic looked embarrassed. She said, "Are you sure?"

The doctor said, "Well I take it that this wasn't planned?" Monic stared at the screen.

Thomas tried to reassure Monic by saying, "No worries. We wanted a large family."

The doctor said, "Then I'll prescribe more vitamin. We can talk about tying your tubes after you give birth."

Monic said, "We'll think about it."

Monic got dressed. Thomas and Monic left the doctor's office. Thomas took her out to lunch. While waiting to order Thomas said, "Baby don't feel bad. You have always been very careful and I appreciate that. That night was beautiful. I feel honored that you let your guard down. This wasn't a mistake. You said you wanted to have children close together."

"Not this close."

"It's alright. We'll just have more love in the house."

"Are you sure?'

"Well it's not like we have a choice."

Monic gave him a look. Thomas took her hands. "There isn't a choice is there?

Monic saw fear and desperation in Thomas' face. She turned her head. The waiter came over. He told them the house specials. The couple had not looked at the menu. They both quickly looked at the menu, thankful for the interruption. The two ordered and the waiter walked away.

Monic's hands were on the table. Thomas put each hand in his. He looked at her. She looked so sad and he saw guilt and regret in her expression. "Baby this is wonderful. Don't turn this blessing into something else. I wouldn't care if you were pregnant with six babies. Monic's expression turned to panic. Thomas smiled. He said, "I love you. These babies were conceived out of love." Monic's expression softened. "I'll help out more so you can get your rest."

"I just don't want to put so much responsibility on you."

"I told you. No worries. We'll be fine. In the past people use to have five or more children and they were fine."

"I just feel irresponsible."

"Am I complaining. This isn't any ones fault. Tyler will have an assortment of who she wants to play with."

"What do you think about me getting my tubes tide?"

"What you don't want any more children? (Thomas smiled) I'm kidding. So are we done?"

"If you don't mind."

"It's fine, but I think I can take care of that."

"What are you saying?"

"I'll get a vasectomy."

"Are you sure?"

"Yes. I mean you've had to have the children."

Monic smiled.

In the coming months Monic did as much as she could to get the center up and running. She occasionally went into the center to make sure everything was running smooth. Monic was placed on bed rest in her seventh month. Her mother-in-law and sister-in-laws pitched in. They came over to watch the children a few hours three times a week.

In Monic's ninth month she had gained a lot of weight. These twins weren't as active as her last.

One morning she arouse early and went to take a shower. Monic was cramping. She entered the shower. As she washed a sharp pain came over her body. She couldn't move. Monic felt a gush. She looked down. Her water had broken. Monic hurried out of the shower. She was able to make it to the bed. Monic layed on the bed, waiting for the pain to subside. After a few minutes Tyler walked into the room. She noticed something was wrong with her mother.

Tyler said, "Hi mommy. Are you ok?"

"Baby I need you to get daddy."

"Ok mommy."

Tyler ran out of the room and down to the kitchen. When she saw Thomas she said, "Daddy mommy wants you."

The look on Tyler's face told him that something was wrong. Thomas turned off the stove and ran up to his room. When he entered the room he saw that Monic was laying on the bed rubbing her stomach. He walked over to Monic.

"What's wrong?"

"My water broke. I'm in a lot of pain."

"I'll call the doctor." (While Thomas called the doctor he gathered clothes for Monic to wear. He helped her put them on. After notifying the doctor that they were on their way he called his mother. She said that she would meet them at the hospital to get the children.

When they arrived at the hospital Thomas' mother and father was waiting in her car. Thomas exited the car and ran into the hospital. When he came out of the hospital he was pushing a wheel chair. His mother and father was removing the children from the car and putting them in theirs. Mrs. Stone told them to go and that they would take the children to her home. As Thomas pushed Monic towards the hospital he looked back and thanked his mother. When they entered the hospital the nurse walked up to them. Monic was taken to the maternity ward. The doctor checked Monic over. She was taken into the birthing room. Just as Monic was moved onto the birthing table she felt a strong urge to push. The doctor instructed her to breathe instead. Once he positioned himself he saw a head. He instructed Monic to push. She pushed twice and the first baby was delivered. Once the baby was given to the nurse the doctor positioned himself again. Monic felt another contraction. After a few pushes, the second baby's head crowned. Monic was instructed to push again. She pushed as hard as she could and the second baby was out. The doctor passed the baby to the nurse. As he turned his attention back to Monic, she got a strong contraction and began to push again. The doctor saw a head emerge. He instructed Monic to push. She did and another baby was born. Thomas looked at the doctor in a questioning manner. The doctor joked by saying, "Mrs. Stone are you done?" Monic looked at the doctor. He said, "I guess we missed one."

Thomas kissed Monic on the forehead.

Monic said, "What did we have?"

The doctor looked at Thomas, smiled and said, "You have two girls and that third one was a boy."

Monic was taken to her room. When the couple was alone Monic said, "Baby what are we going to do?"

"We are going to put Malcolm and Thomas Jr. in the room together and the twins in the room we prepared and our unexpected visitor can go in the upstairs guest room."

"You got it all planned."

"Yes I do. I told you everything will be fine."

"I cant' believe that we have all of these children. I didn't mean for you to be stuck with all of these children."

"Stuck. I don't feel stuck. You shouldn't feel stuck either. Our babies are beautiful. I love them so much and those three in there I can't wait to hold them. Because our children are close in age they are going to always have someone to play with, even if they don't want to. We have enough space in and outside of the house. It's going to be great. I'll help and my parents and sisters will pitch in. You will still be able to work on your project."

Thomas saw some of the tension ease away from Monic's face. Thomas pulled Monic's hands up to his mouth and kissed them. Just then two nurses entered the room pushing their babies. One of the babies was awake. When they came close Monic's heart melted. One of the girls was crying. Monic picked her up. As she held the baby close Monic realized that the baby was hungry. She began to feed the baby.

Thomas said, "When you get home you're going to make as many bottles as you can so you can get some rest. You are not going to be able to breast feed three babies."

"I'll do what I can. If they're anything like the twins I think I will need some help."

The nurse came into the room. She asked for the babies names. Monic said, "This little one here (She was still feeding her son) is Terrance Michael. The little girls who grace us with her presence first is Tory Michelle and the tiny one moving around is Tamara Mac Kayla Stone."

The nurse said, "Those are very beautiful names."

Thomas and Monic said simultaneously, "Thank you."

The nurse said, "I see that you are breast feeding you might want to get other milk because you have three babies. It might be too much."

"My husband and I was just talking about me pumping so he can help."

"That's fine, but depending on the babies appetite, you may not be able to produce enough to feed three."

"I didn't think of that. I thought my body would make as much as I need."

"You also have to think of the demand on your nipples. They may become sore and crack."

"I read about that. I haven't had any of those problems with my twins I pumped and my husband did some of the feeding."

"Well I just wanted you to know your options."

"Thank you."

"I'll leave you with your beautiful babies."

The nurse left. Monic fed the other two babies and then drifted off to sleep. Thomas watched all four while they slept. After some time Terrance woke up. Thomas picked him up. He cleaned his pamper. He held and talked to the baby for a little while. Then he layed him down. Thomas leaned back in his chair and drifted off to sleep.

When Thomas awakened Monic was feeding Tamara. He said, "I forgot to call my mother."

"Call her now. I'm surprised she hasn't called."

Thomas dialed his mother's number. She picked up on the first ring. "Hello."

"Hi Mom."

"Is everything okay?"

"Yes. Everyone is fine."

"I called a hour ago and they said Monic had the baby. They wouldn't tell me anything else. Is Monic alright?"

"Monic and the triplets are fine."

"Triplets? I thought Monic was having twins."

"They didn't see our son."

"Son? You said triplets."

"Monic had two girls and one boy."

"God bless her. When is she getting released?"

"Tomorrow. What you tired of your grandchildren?"

"No. I'm excited. I know they are beautiful."

"Well of course. I am the father."

"I can't believe Monic had triplets. What are you going to do with all those kids?"

"Love and enjoy them."

"Had you planned to have that many kids?"

"No."

"Are you planning to have any more?"

"No. Monic and I talked about it. I'm going to get a vasectomy."

"Are you sure?"

"Yes. Why not? Lord knows I don't need any more kids and why not? Monic had the babies. She shouldn't have to do everything. She made sure all of these years to be careful and didn't get caught out there. Someone should protect her now."

"I am so proud of you. You have grown up to be a good man."

"Why thank you mom."

The next day Monic and the babies were released from the hospital. After they arrived home the babies were placed in their beds. Monic went to lay down. Thomas made an appointment with his doctor to have the procedure done. The next week he called his mother. Within the hour his mother had come over. He helped get the children out of the car. When they entered the house he told Tyler and her siblings that they could see their sisters and brother if they were quiet. The group quietly ascended the stairs.

They entered the girl's room first. The babies were awake. Tyler said, They look alike."

Thomas said, "Yes they do." He pointed to each baby as he told them their names.

Thomas' mother picked up each one and talked to them. She said to Thomas "They are beautiful. You know the girls look like your grandmother."

"I knew they looked like someone, but I couldn't think who."

Just then Tamara began to cry. Thomas picked her up and took her into the room with Monic.

Thomas' mother said, "You don't have any milk made?"

"No. Monic hasn't had a chance to pump any."

Thomas handed Tamara to Monic. Monic adjusted herself. Mrs. Stone went over to Monic and kissed her on the forehead. Mrs. Stone said, "They are beautiful Monic. I'm not going to stay, you need time alone with your family."

"Thank you."

Mrs. Stone left out of the room. She talked to Thomas a while before leaving. After she left Thomas went up to their bedroom. When Thomas entered the room Monic had fallen asleep. The baby was still in her arms and feeding. After the baby seem to have finished Thomas gently took her out of Monic's arms. Monic remained asleep. Thomas checked Tamara's diaper. He changed her. Thomas held Tamara a while before laying her back in the crib. He then went down to the kitchen. Thomas fixed dinner. He fed the older children. After the children had eaten they went into the play room. Thomas gathered the breast pump and made a plate for Monic. He took it up to their room. Monic awakened when Thomas entered the room. She smiled.

She said, "You are so thoughtful."

"I have to take care of my beautiful wife."

Monic sat up. Thomas brought the food over to her. Monic began to eat. The couple talked while Monic ate. After she was done Thomas took the plate and went downstairs. Monic got up and began to use the breast pump. When Thomas returned she was finished. Monic gave the pump and milk to Thomas. She layed back down and soon drifted off to sleep. As she slept Monic dreamed of her mother. Her mother sat next to her. Monic had all of the children next to her. Her mother said, "They are beautiful. I'm sorry I couldn't be here for you, but you'll be alright."

"Mom I miss you."

"And I you. You've grown up beautifully. You did well. I'm proud of you."

"Thank you mom."

Monic hugged her mother. Tears ran down Monic's face. "I wish you could be here mom."

"I'll always be here. You have a good husband. He will take good care of you. Enjoy your family."

Monic woke up.

She had tears in her eyes. She realized Thomas was holding her. As she shifted her body Thomas held her closer. Monic caressed Thomas' arms. She lay there for a few minutes embracing this feeling of security. She drifted off to sleep.

Two hours later she awakened and eased out of Thomas' arms. Monic quietly left the bedroom. She went into Terrance's room. He was awake. Monic changed him and then fed him. As he ate Monic caressed his head. She thought how beautiful he was. Monic thought about her life. She thought of her beginning, before her mother's death. She remembered her mother's touch. Monic remembered the day she was told that her mother had passed. She remembered all of the women who came after her mother. How all of them in their own way protected her. Thomas walked into Terrance room. He saw the tears streaming down Monic's face. He became concerned.

Thomas kneeled down beside Monic. He asked, "What's wrong?"

Monic smoothed her hand over Thomas' face. She smiled and said, "I'm fine. I was just thinking of how blessed I am."

About the Author

My books come from within. They express many of my inner most deepest feelings. I have loved deeply and experienced heart ache that many could not even imagine.

I have been with my one love all of my adult life and would not trade that for anything in the world.